New Beginnings

Susan Schmelzer

Elizabeth Publication
9800 Roberts Rd. S.E.
Galloway, Ohio 43119

New Beginnings

Grateful acknowledgement to my editor, Frances Asbury Pruitt

ISBN: 978-1-7327595-0-3

Chapter 1

She felt deeply conflicted, knowing she was keeping a secret from Travis. Jill had hoped falling in love with the right man would change her desire about not having children. She really did love him. Things have been easing up to visions of romance and together forever.

Jill tried to relax in his arms and brush away thoughts of her secret as Travis leaned down and kissed her cheek, then whispering in her ear, "If everything goes the way I think they will go, it won't be long before we're forever wrapped in each other's arms."

"Oh, Travis, really? Do you mean it?"

Travis, being a few years older, felt optimistic about their future. "Yes, I do. You'll be a college graduate this next spring, and by then I'll have a steady income." Swaying back and forth with her in his arms he continued, "We can pursue our careers, then talk about marriage with a house full of children." Jill's body stiffened when she heard what he said—a house full of children.

Travis turned her toward him. "Did I say something wrong?"

She tossed her hair back from her shoulder and looked up at him. "No, not really; it's just that it's all happening so fast, ending one chapter of our lives and beginning a new one." He'd been talking about children for months, so it wasn't a new thought, but he had never asked her opinion on the subject. She couldn't bring herself to argue the point, not now, and maybe never. What was it about children that he found so appealing? And why couldn't she feel the same way or at least force herself to ask?

Travis pulled her closer to him. "That's the exciting part. Together we'll make new beginnings."

She was quiet as they stood overlooking the pond.

"Jill, look. It's a full moon. The frogs are chirping and the air is calm, so let's get a canoe from the barn and cruise the pond."

"That sounds like fun, especially on my last night at home before heading back to college."

He reached down and took her hand. They walked hand-in-hand to the barn. The moonlight on the water reflected a perfect mirror image of the evening sky. Travis positioned the canoe sideways at the shallow end of the pond. He held onto it with one foot as he reached for Jill's arm.

"Okay, step in the center to keep it balanced."

"O—kay," she replied, with a nervous giggle as she sat toward the front of it.

He pushed the canoe away from the edge and settled in the backseat.

"Have you ever ridden in a canoe before?"

She shook her head. "No, and I don't know how to paddle either. I guess that means you will have to paddle for the two of us."

"Is that what you think?" He began tickling her, causing the canoe to rock.
Laughter was in the air as Jill arched her back. "Travis! Stop tickling me, you're going to make us flip!"

"Hmm, now that's a thought. If a certain someone doesn't want to learn to paddle, maybe she'd rather swim."

"Now, Travis, it's not that I don't want to learn. It's just that…well, it would be more romantic if you do the rowing."

"I can't argue with that. Okay, your wish is my command. It's such a perfect night."

***

Jill unpacked her bags in the house that she called home for the last three years at Malone University. Her thoughts were on what Travis had envisioned about their future. She was thrilled to hear him talk about marriage, but concerned about the mention of children. It sounded like he wanted a lot of them.

How long before he finds out that I don't want children? Then what? I wonder if he would still love me if he knew how I feel—I know he's the one for me! I can't lose him! I won't lose him!

Suddenly she heard a car pull up in front of the house. Excited about seeing one of her roommates, she opened her bedroom window and yelled, "Jackie, you finally made it!"

Jackie eagerly waved as she grabbed the mail out of the mailbox, then rushed toward Jill's room.

Jill flashed a happy smile. "Am I glad to see you, girlfriend!"

Jackie laughed out loud. "This is it! Our last year of college and we will be graduates!"

"Yes, I know," Jill said. "I can't believe it. I am looking forward to start working with my degree in hand!"

Jackie glanced down at the mail in her hand and then waved the top envelope in front of Jill. She smiled. "Here, open it. It's from the university. Hurry, read it!"

Jill grabbed the envelope, looked it over, then excitedly half-whispered, "It's from the dean's office." She quickly ripped it open and with a shaky voice read out aloud:

"Dear Jillian,

We would like to congratulate you on receiving the highest scores in Journalism during your junior year at Malone University. Enclosed you will find one ticket and one backstage pass to the Winter Runway Fashion Show in New York."

In disbelief Jill screamed, "What? Oh my goodness!" She was sitting on the edge of her bed when she leaped to her feet. "I can't believe it! I'm going to New York! I'm going to New York!" With the letter in her hand, she grabbed Jackie and hugged her.

That night after she journaled in bed, Jill laid her pen down and thought, *Oh, there is so much to think about: the Davenport Derby, memorizing a new class schedule, looking for a job, Homecoming, and now the New York trip during the holidays.*

*I can't wait to tell Travis the good news. Wait a minute…*she pushed back her covers, hopped out, and went to study her calendar on her desk. *Let's see, when did Travis say he would be going to New York if everything goes well with his proposed doll line?*

Flipping to the month of December, she saw where she had penciled in the week before Christmas. Travis was to fly out to New York and return the following Sunday. *Oh wait, what are the dates for the fashion show?* She reached over to her nightstand where she'd laid the dean's letter. It was the Saturday before Travis would fly home. *I need to get online first thing in the morning and see if I can schedule a flight out on that Saturday so I can fly back home with Travis on Sunday.* She tucked the letter back into the envelope, eager to get to bed. New beginnings were already in motion.

Chapter 2

An early riser, Jill hummed in the kitchen while she filled the coffee maker with water. While waiting for the coffee to brew, she decided to search the web for the best-priced airline tickets to New York.

Without warning Jackie said, "Good morning!"

Jill glanced over toward Jackie heading straight for the coffeepot. "Hey there, Jackie." Jill was about to tell Jackie about her conversation with Travis the night before, but decided she wasn't ready to defend her desire to remain childless.

"What time did Sadie and Tara come in last night?"

Jackie yawned as she grabbed two coffee mugs off the rack and filled them.

"Around twelve-thirty, I think. They came into my room all excited about the school's Davenport Derby competition this Thursday."

Jill, still studying her computer screen, replied, "Oh yeah? What's the plan? Do we have a theme picked out?"

Jackie sat down at the table and set a cup in front of Jill. "They're thinking we could do the Flintstones theme, making a paper mache' Fred the driver. You and I will ride on the loveseat as Pebbles and Bamm-Bamm, and Sadie and Tara will push us during the race."

Jill visualized it all as she slowly nodded in agreement. She took a sip of her coffee and happily set down her cup. "It sounds like a good plan to me. The loveseat would be the right size for a Flintstone car and make it easier for the two of them to push us. I want to be Pebbles."

Jackie shrugged her shoulders. "I knew you would. Okay, I'll be Bamm-Bamm. Tara and Sadie can be Betty and Wilma."

The two of them sat and drank their coffee, discussing their outfits for the derby.

When Jill noticed the sunbeam shining through the kitchen door window, she abruptly jumped to her feet. "Oh, I'd better get going! I have a lot to do today, and I can't wait to talk to Travis, and tell him everything that's happened. See ya."

Jackie grinned and waved. "See ya later."

Chapter 3

The scent of autumn was in the air, Jill's favorite season in Ohio. With thoughts of leaves turning vivid colors, and low humidity, Jill knew this would be a great day. And because of low humidity, she could wear her long dark hair with its natural curl straight, just the way Travis liked it.

Jill felt the warmth of the sun on her face. Dressed in knee-high cranberry boots and a cable-knit sweater with a matching scarf, she had nearly reached the campus office when she ran into her longtime friend.

"Hey Brad, are you headed over to sign up for Thursday's Davenport Derby?"

"No, but thanks for the reminder. I heard there's a big manufacturing company in town hiring college students. I'm on my way over to read the post on the community board, then I'm driving over there to put in my application."

Jill's eyes grew wide with excitement. "Really? Can I go with you? I need to get a job right away, so I can meet my goal of paying off my loans by the time I graduate."

Brad smiled. "Same here. You know how our parents drilled that into us before we left home."

Jill chuckled. "It's funny that not only did we grow up together, but we ended up at the same college, and now we're both applying for jobs at the same company."

Brad smiled, and agreed to take her along. As they were driving, Jill's mind was on a caffeine high, once again haunted by the secret she was keeping from Travis. She asked Brad. "I have a hypothetical question for you."

"Okay, shoot."

"If you were dating a girl who told you she didn't want to have children, how would you respond?"

Taken aback by the question, Brad stuttered. "Wha…well, hmm. It would depend on her reasoning."

Jill snapped. "Brad!"

"What? I need an answer. What would be her reason?"

"Okay, let's just say she was afraid of childbearing. Or maybe, worried about losing her figure, or getting stretch marks."

Brad frowned and shook his head. "Well, those are pretty shallow reasons to not want children."

Jill argued. "Why would you think that?"

"She's only thinking about herself. Hypothetically speaking, she could research ways to minimize those issues."

She slumped down in her seat and snapped, "Oh, you would say that."

He smiled. "What is this all about anyway—a school paper? From an engineer's point of view, I assume you're looking for a more mature non-biased prospective." The conversation ended as they pulled into the parking lot.

Chapter 4

Travis yawned as he stood up from his computer desk. He looked at his watch, surprised to realize he'd been sitting so long.

I wonder what Jill is doing? He reached for his phone and texted her. "Are you free to talk?" His phone dinged a reply instantly.

"Almost, I'll call you as soon as I'm free. I have so much to tell you."

Hmm, okay. I wonder what she's doing, he thought, as he went to the kitchen and grabbed a banana and a jar of peanut butter. For the past year he had put a lot of hours into the design of his new product line and was almost finished. Soon he would be able to present it to a production company. After he finished eating he headed outdoors to his family's equestrian facility, Faith Ridge Farm.

On his walk to the barn he thought back to when Jill introduced him to peanut butter on pancakes. It was New Year's morning when his mother, Bobby Sue, offered the original farmhouse to the college Bible study group to celebrate New Year's Eve. The house had been a bed and breakfast run by his grandparents when his mother was a child.

They had stayed up all night playing in the snow and enjoying games in the house, until they finally crashed, with the girls sleeping upstairs and the guys sacking out on the lower level. The next day they woke to the aroma of bacon, egg casserole, maple syrup, and pancakes. Jill had asked Bobby Sue if she could have peanut butter for her pancakes.

Travis frowned in confusion. "Did you just ask for peanut butter?"

Jill felt silly when she took the peanut butter jar from Bobby Sue. "I did. I love peanut butter on my pancakes. You should try it." She grabbed a spoonful of peanut butter and suddenly stuck it to the end of Travis's nose.

He looked cross-eyed down at the spoon hanging off his nose. "Oh! You really didn't just do that!"

Jill giggled as she reached for the spoon. "Oops, I meant to put it in your mouth."

Travis grabbed her wrist and pulled her toward him, then he picked her up and turned her upside down and held her by her ankles.

Jill screamed as she tried to wiggle out of his grasp. "Travis! Put me down!"

He leaned forward. "What? Jill, I don't understand you." Everyone at the table laughed.

Travis loved the way she always made him laugh with her child-like charm. It was like a stress release from his work. He smiled at the memory as he approached the barn.

There was Oscar, the old family horse that he and his sister started out on as a 4-H project. Their mother volunteered as an equestrian advisor for the club while he showed Oscar in Western and Trail classes, along with his younger sister, Greta, adding English and Jumping. He loved this horse. Oscar was an old foundation quarter horse that would do anything for you with a willing heart. His bay color had white markings; a white blaze that ran down between his big brown eyes and one white ankle.

Oscar greeted Travis at the window of his stall.

"Hey, buddy, how's it going?" Oscar nickered and lifted his head so Travis could rub under his jaw. Travis smiled as he rubbed the horse's favorite spot. "Would you like to go check on some 'Have-a-Heart' traps with me?"

Even though it wasn't trapping season, Travis had applied for a nuisance tag for a family of raccoons that kept tearing things up at the equestrian facility. Oscar's ears perked up as Travis chuckled. "Ok, buddy, let's get you out." With a hackamore, reins, and a leap onto Oscar's back, the two of them were off to the pond area.

They passed the outdoor arena filled with a group of orphans in a class taught by his sister, Greta, who waved at him as they trotted by. By nature, Travis loved to be outside more than inside. Growing up on a horse farm and being home schooled, he had a lot of opportunities to enjoy God's creations. His mom always teased him that he would turn into some sort of amphibian from hanging out so often at the pond and creek beds.

For as long as he could remember he had always had an aquarium in his bedroom. His office even housed a fifty-five-gallon aquarium that Jill had put her claim on. Every time she came home from college she would sweet talk him into buying a new fish to put in it. A week before she left, she and Travis went to the pet store and picked out a polka-dotted fish. To their surprise it ended up being full of eggs. So now Travis has a huge school of polka-dotted fish in his tank.

As Travis approached the pond, he tried to see how close he could get to the frogs before they hopped into the water from the edge.

He had named the oldest bullfrog in the pond Big Buford. He loved to catch him whenever he saw him out basking in the sun. Travis shifted his body weight down into his seat, leaned back slightly, taking his leg pressure off the sides of Oscar, and cued him to whoa. Momentarily he slid off the rump of the ol' boy. He crunched down and slowly made his way toward Big Buford. He could still see the old scars on Buford's back. Years earlier during the time the pond was being built, Travis had witnessed a sheep's foot crush Buford's back right leg. Travis had run down into the base of the pond and gently picked up the frog. Somehow he convinced his mom to take Buford to the local vet to see if his leg could be saved.

Travis's mind came back to focus, trying to determine whether Buford was asleep on the rock. With its three legs poised over the edge of the rock, he could see that this was the moment to leap. Swish went Travis's hands as he leaped toward the rock and scooped up the bullfrog in one swoop. Big Buford let out a loud squelch that made Travis feel like a young boy again. He grinned from ear to ear as he looked back at Oscar. "I've still got it, ol' buddy!" Oscar flickered his ears toward him without a lift of his head from grazing.

Travis was amazed that the three-legged bullfrog had survived all those years. "Well, buddy, I hope the good Lord gives you another eighteen years here." With that he put him back on his rock.

Chapter 5

Quite a few college students were in the room filling out applications. Jill leaned over to Brad and whispered, "Do you think they'll hire us?"

Brad inhaled a deep breath of Jill's perfume. "With your personality," he assured her, "if you get an interview, you'll be secured a position."

She leaned back in her seat, wrinkled her nose, and smiled at him, unaware that his heart skipped a beat or two every time he was around her. It started back to their elementary school days. Jill, wearing a frilly dress and a big bow in her hair, would pass out milk cartons during snack time and curtsy at the boys with a shy giggle. Nor could she imagine that he could still feel the way his cheeks grew warm every time she'd walked past him.

Brad cleared his throat. "I'll be right back," he said. As he walked over to get a drink from the water fountain, the lady at the desk called Jill's name.

Jill sprang from her seat and looked around for Brad. Their eyes met as she held up crossed fingers and went into the interview. Brad winked back at her. Later he told her that he had prayed, *if it's Your will, Lord, let her get a position where she can shine for You. Amen,* adding, and that when they called his name he also prayed, *Oh, and me too, Lord.*

During Jill's interview she explained that she was getting a dual degree in HR and journalism. She loved to travel, give demonstrations, make up schedules, create employee profiles, and work with people. At the end of the interview she stood up, shook the lady's hand, and thanked her for considering her application. Then she added that she looked forward to hearing from her soon.

Brad was sitting in the lobby when she walked out from her interview. "Hey, how did it go?"

"I have a good feeling about it!" Jill was so pumped telling him all about the interview that she didn't even ask him if he'd had his interview yet.

"Are you ready to go?" Brad asked as he stood up.

"Yep, I'm all set," Jill replied, then added, "Oh, wait…I'm sorry, did you already have an interview?"

"Yes, I did. Apparently I wasn't as windy as you." He nudged her with his elbow.

She pushed him backward and whispered in annoyance, "Brad!"

As they drove back to campus, Jill noticed a smoothie shop. "Oh Brad, let's stop and get a smoothie! My treat. I mean after all, you did drive."

Brad swung into the turn lane with a tease in his voice, "Yeah, even after you invited yourself."

Jill looked surprised, then whispered, "Well, maybe I did, but that's beside the point."

Chapter 6

Back at the pond, Travis walked softly over to the edge of the woods and looked toward his "Have-a-Heart Traps." Sure enough he'd caught the whole gang of raccoons.

I'll have to come back with the Jeep to relocate them to the creek, he thought. Just then his phone chirped. Pulling it out of his pocket, he saw that it was Jill. He walked back toward Oscar as he answered.

"Hey Jill. How are you?"

"I'm great! You'll never guess what I've been doing!"

Travis reclined on the hillside beside Oscar and sighed aloud, "Am I supposed to guess?"

"Yes, but let me give you a few clues. It has something to do with my future and my passion."

Travis leaned up on his elbows with the speakerphone on and jokingly asked, "You got a job at a smoothie shop?"

"Travis!" Jill huffed. "No! I'm not going to college to work at a smoothie shop. Really, do you even consider that a career job?"

"Well, yes I do. To be a manager it does take some schooling and—"

Jill interrupted, "Oh, Travis, never mind. I had an interview with a big manufacturing corporation today!"

"Wow, you did?"

She continued, "Yes, and do you know what else?"

He hesitated. "Hmm…do you want me to guess again?"

She sighed aloud. "No. Anyway I was awarded a ticket to a fashion show! I am going to New York during the holidays. I had hoped we could see a little bit of New York together and...."

Travis interrupted, "Hold on, hold on! You won tickets to a fashion show in New York? How?"

"Well, just one ticket and yes it's in New York! Travis, I earned the highest honors in my journalism class last year and they rewarded me with this rare opportunity!"

"Wow! Congratulations, Jill! I'm proud of you!"

She squealed. "Thank you! Anyway, when can you come up to see me? We have to make a detailed plan in order to meet in New York."

"I'm not sure just yet. I have a conference call set up for Friday, and with our Gymkhana show this Saturday my parents asked if I would be the arena judge for them. So that leaves Sunday. Hey, why don't we meet halfway and talk about it over a nice dinner?"

She was quiet for a long minute.

"Jill, are you there?"

"Yes, I'm here. Travis, do you really have to judge the horse show on Saturday? Can't your friend Jack do it?

"Jack is going to help Greta with a group of orphan kids who will be competing."

"Hmm, well then, I want to choose the place where we should meet. How about the Olive Garden?"

"It sounds like a plan to me. Hey, I gotta go. What time on Sunday do you want to meet?"

She thought for a moment. "How about four o'clock? That will give us plenty of time to get home from church, hang out, and talk after dinner before we part ways. Maybe we can even get a smoothie afterwards."

Travis chuckled. "You and your smoothies. But it sounds good. I'll call you tonight."

"Okay, yeah, I have to meet my roomies soon. We're going to get our costumes for the Davenport Derby on Thursday. Hint, hint, maybe you could come up on Thursday and surprise me?" She couldn't see him shake his head with a half of a smile as he said, Bye, Jill.

Chapter 7

Derby Day! Jill and her roommates were excited about getting dressed and going over to Brad's frat house to see how their loveseat assembly was going. The girls had bought two-by-fours, wheels, and screws. Brad assured them that he and his roommates would put a sturdy brace on their loveseat in time for the race.

Jackie pulled the last batch of chocolate chip cookies out of the oven to take to the boys as a payment for their help. The room smelled delicious after her fourth batch. Sadie and Tara came into the kitchen amazed at the mound of cookies Jackie had piled up.

She smiled at them as she carried the last tray over to the table. "Oh good, you two can help package these cookies for the guys."

Sadie spoke first as she grabbed a cookie from the top. "Sure! They probably won't mind if I eat one."

Tara chimed in as she snatched one too. "Yeah, we have to make sure they're edible."

Just then Sadie looked around. "Hey, where's Jill?"

"You know Jill," Jackie replied, "She's upstairs coordinating our Flintstone costume with the right hair accessories, nail polish, and jewelry."

The girls laughed and Tara added, "Yes, she's all about that. She's really good when it comes to fashion."

The theme song to the Laverne and Shirley TV show started to play. "Oh! That's my phone." Tara answered, "Hello? Oh hey, Brad. Yes, Jill is here. She is upstairs doing what she does best. Yep, you got it, fashion girl at play. Okay, yep, hold on, I'll yell for her."

Tara put her hand over the phone and yelled for Jill as she walked toward the stairs.

Jill ran from her bedroom to the top of the stairway. "What?"

Tara held the phone out toward Jill. "It's Brad. He said you didn't answer your phone."

Jill looked with a frown toward her bedroom. "Oh shoot, I'll bet I forgot to turn up the volume after I got up this morning. I hope I didn't miss a call from Travis. Okay, tell him I'll call him back in about ten minutes."

Tara put the phone to her ear and heard him say, "I heard. Okay, Thanks."

"I wish Brad would call for me just once," Tara mumbled as she walked back into the kitchen.

Sadie looked at her with a sad smile on her face. "Oh, there are lots of fish in the sea. My mother always told me it's better to have a long-time friendship then a two-week boyfriend."

Jill rushed into the kitchen. "Hey girls, I already laid out everything we're going to wear to the race today. I'm so excited! I can hardly wait." She looked at Tara and asked, "Did Brad tell you what he wanted?"

Tara looked up from where she was about to grab another cookie from the pile. "Um, no, but I think it's about our loveseat brace."

"Yes, you're probably right. When do you girls want to go over and help?"

Jackie spoke up first. "Hey, I'm done making cookies. Once they're packaged I'll be ready to go."

Tara nodded. "I should check in with the drama team to see what time play rehearsal will be, due to the race today."

Sadie continued, "We also need to stop by the art department and pick up our cardboard Flintstone car wheels. Oh, and Fred. He looks so real with the wig we added to his paper mache head."

Jill giggled at the mental image in her head. "We can only hope his wig doesn't fly off at the speed we'll be racing."

They all laughed before Jill added, "We should leave no later than ten minutes from now. That should give us plenty of time to swing by and pick everything up."

***

As the girls pulled up to Brad's place, they gasped in awe of the guys' Batman couch. Sadie was the first to jump out of the car and compliment Brad's roommates—Tim, Tom, and Mark—on their creation. They had hung Batman emblems on the front and back of the couch.

She grinned. "This looks awesome, guys!"

"Thanks." They replied in unison.

The other girls strolled up as Brad walked out of the house. "Hey, Jill, it's about time you got here. Still pondering our discussion from the other day?"

Jill tilted her head to one side and studied his face. "I'd rather not go there." She found a toss pillow and pitched it at him for good measure.

Chapter 8

When Jill called, Travis was contemplating his schedule: Friday night's conference call with his childhood friend and business partner, Jonah, along with the trade show organizer in Tennessee; judge the Gymkhana show all day on Saturday, then meet Jill on Sunday.

"Hi, Travis, you still have time to drive up to see me as Pebbles."

"I wish I could but it's a two-and-a-half hour trip up to Canton. I really don't want to drive five hours for such a short visit. Remember, I have an important conference call tomorrow that requires my undivided attention before it happens. How about you ask someone to record it and send it to me?"

"Okay, I understand. It's just that I have the cutest Pebbles outfit and I wanted you to see me in it."

Travis laughed softly. "Jill, I have no doubt that you will be the cutest Pebbles ever, and I wish I could be there to cheer you on. By the way, did Brad get the brace done for your loveseat?"

"Yes, he did, and I'm going to beat him in the derby!"

Travis chuckled as he ended the call hoping that her team would beat Brad's team.

***

Jill, determined not to be depressed that Travis couldn't come, thought a smoothie would be just what she needed.

After she hung up the phone, she said, "Hey guys, let's go get a smoothie before we push these couches to the Derby. I need a little sugar before I get into character and costume."

All the guys moaned agreeing that they had eaten too many cookies. They also accused her that it was a ploy to get them sick on sugar so they would lose the race.

However, Tara cheerfully spoke up. "I'll go with you."

Sadie and Jackie elected to stay behind to strap the paper mache Fred Flintstone into their loveseat and watch over it so no one would sabotage it before the race.

Brad looked at them with disbelief. "What? Really? Who do you think put your wheels and bracing on your loveseat?"

Sadie smiled as she walked up to Brad. "You!" She pushed her index finger into his chest. "And that's exactly why I am staying here."

Jackie chimed in, "Yeah, and I'm going to check out all your handy work too, son."

Jill and Tara walked toward the car, convinced that it was a good idea that the girls were staying with their derby couch.

As they drove to the smoothie shop, Tara asked, "Jill, how would you feel if I began to pursue a relationship with Brad?"

Jill's jaw dropped as she looked at Tara. "Seriously? I mean, you have a thing for Brad? How long have you had this mad crush on him?"

Tara was a little embarrassed to admit, "Since we played opposite each other in 'Bye Bye Birdie' last spring. I've thought about him all summer. The way his voice is so incredibly dreamy and Jill, he looked so handsome in that black leather jacket. Today he'll be wearing a tight black leather Batman costume. I can hardly wait to see him in it." Tara let out an audible sigh. "He drives me crazy and he doesn't even know it!"

Jill didn't know what to think or say as they pulled up to the drive-thru window. "Oh, Tara, girl, you really have it bad for him!"

***

Jill parked the car at the curb in front of Brad's frat house. Sadie and Brad were still going at it over the quality of the couch brace.

Jill approached them frowning. "Are you two still at it? Come on, you guys. You act like an old married couple."

She'd scarcely finished speaking before she saw the look on Tara's face. It clearly demanded that she keep her mouth shut and say nothing about her feelings for Brad.

Brad threw his hands in the air in frustration as he walked toward Jill. "Oh, I see how it is. Work a man to death but don't give him any gratitude for all his effort!"

Jill put on a pouty face and teased, "What? Little Brad couldn't handle Sadie while we were gone?"

"That does it!" Brad argued. "Competition is on! I was helping out of the kindness of my heart, but now, whichever team wins this derby has to push the other team's couch back home!"

The girls looked at each other grinning and agreed hands down that they would reap the reward.

Chapter 9

Everyone was anxious to start the derby race. The announcer said that the skits would be first. Once they judged the skits, the race would begin. The female dorms/homes would start the race, followed by the male dorms/homes. Once the scores were added together, the top female and male winner would compete for the school title.

Jill as Pebbles, Jackie as Bamm-Bamm, Sadie as Wilma, and Tara as Betty were up next with the Flintstone song and drill.

The girls were hyped as they waited to compete in the foot race against the cheerleaders. Their theme was "Carrie, on Prom Night." Jill talked over their strategies: Sadie, as the most athletic one, elected to push the loveseat first in hopes it would give them a lead in the race. Tara would push from the side rail and wave to the crowd to keep them pumped up. Jackie would beat the couch with her club, then wave the club in the air while Jill would be her cute little Pebbly self, doing baby dance moves. Once they crossed the line, Sadie would grab the side rail and Tara would push from behind, back up the 1000-feet lane to the starting line to complete the race. The girls beat the cheerleaders by half a couch cushion with a score of fifty-seven seconds.

Then it was time to watch Brad's Batman team race. They made it in forty-eight seconds. This beat the girls' time but not the team they raced against, so they were knocked out of the competition. Now it was up to the last girls' team to see if Jill's team would race the fastest guy team. It was "Chick-fil-A" against the "Donatos' Pizza" delivery girls. Everyone cheered for their favorite team. "Chick-fil-A" won by two-tenths of a second against Jill's team.

"Oh no!" Jill said to the girls. "Oh well, I think we were the cutest!"

Jackie started chanting. "Bamm-Bamm, we were the cutest! Bamm-Bamm, we were the cutest!"

Brad, Tim, Tom, and Mark walked cockily toward them, Brad wearing a smirk on his face. "Yeah, well cute won't get you out of paying up on the bet we made."

Jill batted her Pebble eyes at Brad. "You're really not going to make us push the couch back to your house, are you?"

Brad looked Jill up and down in her baby doll outfit, turned to his roommates, and sighed quietly, "Help me out here guys. I can't hold the line without you."

Just then Tim, Tom, and Mark stepped forward pushing Brad behind them.

Tom spoke up. "You're not going to charm your way out of this one, Jill, or any of you girls!"

"Yeah, a deal is a deal!" Tim added. "So let's get pushin', ladies."

The girls frowned in annoyance as they made their way to the Batmobile to push it back to Brad's frat house.

Brad flashed a cold smirk and added. "We'll see you girls at the cookout—if you arrive before it's over. Oh listen, don't forget to push your Flintstone car home too, or it will be considered littering if you leave it in the parking lot after today."

Once the girls finished removing the couches, they drove to the campus grounds where the school held a cookout for the race participants. Tara spotted Brad first and whispered to Jill, "Hey Jill, tell me, how should I handle my Brad situation?"

"Well, let's see...you're in the school play with him, right?"

"Yes, he has the lead part in Oklahoma. He's Curly."

"And what's your part?"

"Well, I'm a dancer. I missed the tryouts for Annie so, of course, the captain of the cheerleading squad got the part. But I know every one of her songs, and I'm going to approach the drama teacher about letting me be the understudy if she can't make it for some reason. Maybe he'll have me rehearse with Brad a few times just so I'll know her lines."

Jill grinned from ear to ear. "Tara, babe, I think you're very clever in this high pursuit of a man thing!" They laughed so hard they didn't notice Brad when he walked up to them.

"Do you wanna clue me in on the joke?"

Startled, Jill spoke up first. "Nope, no can do!"

Tara blushed as she asked if she could get a ride to play rehearsal if he was going that way.

"That would be fine," he answered. "Just meet me at the ice cream table in an hour."

Chapter 10

Jill woke up to the sound of one of her roommates' screaming. "What! Oh no, they didn't!"

With a flip of her covers, Jill was out of bed in a heartbeat and running down the stairs. "What? What is going on?"

In the kitchen Tara and Sadie stood at Jackie's shoulder as she sat at her computer staring at the screen. There in living color was a full-size picture of them pushing the Batmobile down the street. Jill couldn't believe it was plastered all over the school's Facebook page.

"Brad! Oh!" She stomped her foot, turned, and shook her finger at the girls. "You just wait, girls. We'll get them back! I don't know how yet, but I assure you we will!"

Suddenly Tara's phone went off. She stepped away from the computer and grabbed it off the kitchen counter. "Oh, speak of the devil himself—he just sent me a text."

"Tara," the text read, "The drama teacher called me this morning and said he'd like to offer you the understudy part playing Annie. I agreed with him that it was a good idea. Can you meet at the auditorium in an hour?"

"Eek! Yes, I can!" Tara squealed excitedly.

All her roommates turned and looked at her. "Yes, you can what?" Jackie asked.

Sadie ran over to her. "Who texted you and what are you so excited about?"

Tara held her phone to her heart. "I get to meet Brad in an hour and rehearse with him as the understudy for the part of Annie!"

Jill's mouth dropped open. "What? You got the part of Annie?"

Tara shook her head. "No. Well, not yet." She began pacing the room. "That would only happen if for some reason the girl playing Annie can't make it.

But I get to rehearse with Brad just in case." The girls all gathered in a group hug showing her their support.

***

The next hour zoomed past for Tara, who had to shower before riding her bike to the school auditorium. Her heart pounded harder the closer she got to the door. She could hear Brad bellow the song, "Oh, What a Beautiful Morning!" She opened the door slowly and carefully so she didn't interrupt the moment, then took a seat in the back row. When Brad finished his song the first few rows of cast members clapped and whistled. Tara got up from her seat and joined them.

Mr. Hook, the music director, looked up and smiled, "Ah, there you are. Good morning, Tara, and thank you for coming."

"You're welcome, Mr. Hook."

"Okay, Brad, are you ready to sing 'People Will Say We're In Love' with Tara? I'd like to hear the harmony between you two."

"Yes sir, I am." Brad looked over at Tara with a soft smile and mouthed the word, "Ready?" She shyly smiled and nodded yes. A stage crew tied a scarf around her neck and handed Brad some fake flowers to hold behind his back as they pushed a glider on stage for them to sit on.

"Okay, Tara, you and Brad will come in from stage left as you hold hands," Mr. Hook instructed. "I want you to gaze into each other's eyes. Tara, you'll be on Brad's right. You'll stop in front of the glider and Brad will pull out the flowers. He will take both your hands together so that all four hands hold the flowers. That's when the music will start. I want to see improvisation from both of you while you sing. Make sure the song ends with both of you sitting side by side on the glider. Oh, and Brad, once you are on the glider," he added, "I want your arm around her shoulders. The stage lights will go black as the music ends. Do either of you have any questions?"

Brad nodded. "I think I've got it."

Tara could feel the tightness in her throat and knew that her neck was red with anticipation as to what was about to play out.

"No, sir." she replied nervously.

"Okay then, let's do this. Places everyone."

After the song, Mr. Hook smiled. "I'm very pleased with the chemistry between the two of you," He said. "Tara, the way you carried yourself through the song made me feel as though you were really in love. You were like butter in Curly's arms. That was quite impressive. And you harmonized beautifully together. Well done."

Tara floated out of the auditorium on cloud nine. She couldn't wait for the next practice.

Chapter 11

Travis called Jill on his lunch break from the Gymkhana show. "Hey, how are you doing?"

"Oh, Travis! Have you looked on Facebook today?"

"No, I haven't. I've been busy with the horse show."

"Well, you won't believe what Brad did!"

"Okay, tell me, what did Brad do?"

"He plastered a picture on the school's Facebook page of us barely able to push the Batmobile down the street with a caption of 'The Flintstones have attitude and with the future.'"

Travis tried to visualize Jill in her Pebbles outfit pushing the Batmobile. "Well, Jill, take it with a grain of salt. It is Brad, you know."

Jill's voice rose in her defense. "Exactly! That's why I'm going to get him back!"

"Oh, I'm sure you will. But hey, the reason I called, I wanted to tell you I got an email confirming that I will have my patent in hand by the time I go to the production company in New York. Also, Gary wants me to fly down to Tennessee and meet with him about my runway show proposal in person."

Jill interrupted. "Wait, who's Gary?"

"He's the CEO of the toy trade shows. He liked my idea of a runway show as part of the marketing for my doll line."

Jill's emotions were full of excitement for Travis. "Oh, I'm really happy for you! This is going to be big! I'll start to work on the color scheme for the skirt and drapery for the stage."

"Okay, that sounds good. Hey, I have to get back to the horse show. They're starting the team events. I'll see you tomorrow."

Chapter 12

Jill was anxious to see Travis. She walked into Olive Garden feeling confident, decked out in a pink tunic, dark gray skinny jeans, gray ankle boots with a bow on the side, a long pearl necklace, with a Coach purse in hand.

"You would make a beautiful model for my doll collection," he said. As they embraced, he added, "Mmm you smell good!"

"Thanks," Jill answered. "It's Calvin Klein." Then she asked, "Where are we sitting?"

Travis stepped back and led her to a table. As they ate, Jill shared about her job interview. With excitement in her voice, she added that they called and told her that the job was hers if she wanted it.

Travis was delighted with the news, but added, "I hope you can work the travel in with your school schedule."

After dinner Jill talked Travis into a trip to the smoothie shop to get a mango, papaya, strawberry and banana smoothie. On the way Travis talked about his business itinerary that was scheduled. Jill, very career oriented, loved to talk about business. That was one thing they had in common.

Sitting outside on the patio at the smoothie shop, Travis shared ideas about how to make a difference in an orphan's life. "I came up with a way to raise money for orphan children…a way to better their future."

Jill stopped in a middle of a slurp and met his gaze. "Really? Tell me about it."

Travis cleared his throat. "Okay, you know how Jonah and I have a design patent where we take a person's photo and mold it into a doll's face?" Jill nodded. Travis continued, "We'll select an orphan's profile and their story to make a numbered collector's doll. Every customer who purchases a doll will have an ongoing opportunity to donate money into a private trust fund set-up for that particular orphan. The doll will be packaged with that child's story. This will give the buyers a way to connect with them, not only financially but emotionally, as well. The money collected will go toward education or other ways to enhance their future. They can even encourage their children to forego a gift during the holidays in order to add money to their doll's account."

Jill processed it all as she continued to slurp the last of her smoothie, then she exclaimed. "What a great way to teach children about giving at a young age."

"It will give people opportunities to help orphans better themselves when they're not in a position to provide them a home. I love the fact that we can design a look-a-like doll to make each one feel special, to let them know they are not some anonymous face lost in the crowd."

She was in awe of his ideas.

He continued, "I know there will always be children who live as orphans since there aren't enough families who can adopt them all. If we have the opportunity to offer hope to as many as we can, then we should!"

She loved the compassion that Travis felt toward children. It was bittersweet, though, because she knew deep down in her heart that she did not want to physically have children of her own. This was something she had not shared with him, as the issue had derailed previous relationships in the past.

"Speaking of orphan kids, you should have seen the ones my mom brought to the horse show yesterday. They had so much fun being outdoors with the horses and playing games. They were worn out by the time we took them back to the orphanage. I can't wait to have children someday."

Travis took her hands into his as he leaned toward her, "Jill, I have something to ask you."

All of a sudden her heart started to beat harder, anticipating his next words. *What? Wait, Now? Is he going to ask me to marry him? Oh, oh, um…*

Travis turned her hands over and rubbed his thumbs over the palm of her hands. "Jill...why are your hands so sweaty?"

She looked down at her hands and with a soft giggle she lifted her shoulders and looked up at him.

"Is... this what I think this is?"

Travis looked at her with his head tilted, as puppy dogs do when they're confused by a command.

He frowned. "Is this what?"

Oh no! It's not what I was thinking. Oh, I feel so stupid!

Travis shook his head, dismissing the confusion. "I wanted to ask you, how many children do you see in your future?"

Jill's eyes widened, stunned by the one and only question she never wanted to answer. She swallowed hard, unsure what to say. All she knew was that this wasn't a proposal and she certainly didn't want to admit that she didn't want to have children.

"Hmm." She cleared her throat. "Well…… I don't know…. That's a loaded question and it's so far into the future." She did her best to avoid giving him a direct answer, before rambling on. "Right now I have my focus on my last year of college and finding a career job."

He looked surprised by her response. "Yes, I guess it is a loaded question, but it's not that far off in the future. I mean, I'm hard at work to set up my finances now and for my future. I have several rental properties and I'm nearly ready to go into production of my doll line and get approval for the orphans' trust foundation, so marriage and children don't seem far off to me."

Jill, focusing on her own views about children, lost her concentration.

He went on. "When I'm around those orphaned kids, it makes me anxious to have my own."

She started to feel overly warm inside, but not the fuzzy warmth that Travis' was describing. Yearning to get up and run away, she abruptly pulled away from him. "I have to go to the ladies' room."

She leaped to her feet and hurried toward the restrooms where she grabbed some paper towels and ran cold water over them. Lifting the hair off the back of her neck, she placed the wet towels on her skin. With her eyes closed she inhaled, wondering how she would escape his probing question. Closing her eyes, she tried to relax, but her mind raced.

She thought back to the time when she was three years old and her sister was born. The truth was that she never liked sharing the spotlight with her sister. *Does that make me a selfish person? Is what Brad said true about the scenario I gave him? Am I selfish, or just afraid of the unknown?* She re-dampened the paper towels and pressed them to the back of her neck, thinking she had never really played with her younger cousins at family gatherings either. She studied her reflection in the mirror, and tried to make sense of her feelings.

Maybe I was too mature for my age. I've always preferred to hang out with the adults at family gatherings. Ugh, what is wrong with me? She gathered the wet paper towels and tossed them into the trash can, then fixed her hair. *I better get back out there or Travis will have the waitress come in to check on me.*

Jill walked outside to the patio where she felt she could breathe again, pulled out her chair and sat down. She glanced up at Travis and apologized for her behavior. She could tell he was concerned.

"Are you okay? What just happened?"

Jill gave him a distraught look and blurted, "Travis, I don't want to have children." There—she'd said it, without meaning to. It just happened. She held her breath as she studied his face. He looked like a deer caught in headlights.

"No children? None at all? Really? You're kidding me, right?"

She continued. "No, Travis, I'm not kidding you. I wouldn't joke about something like this. I've never had the desire to have children. I don't like drool, poo, or crying."

"You're serious? Wow!" He pushed away from the table and stood with his hands on his hips, looking long and hard at her, in total disbelief. She sat quietly then watched him exit the food court, as if he couldn't believe his ears.

Jill wiped the tears from her eyes as she saw him turn and walk back toward her.

"I've never heard of someone who didn't want children. I've heard of some who were unable to have them, but—really? That's how you really feel?"

Jill started to panic. *Oh no, not again, I'm going to lose Travis, too!* She looked up at him. "Will you sit down so we can talk about this?"

He pulled out his chair and plopped down.

She knew by the way he reacted that she had to come up with a strong definitive answer and a good reason.

"Well, as you just mentioned, there are other ways to include children in your life, including fostering, adoption, signing up to be a big brother or a big sister, or even finding someone to be a surrogate mother."

Travis leaned forward with his hands folded in front of him on the table. "So, you're saying you don't want to physically go through labor to have children, but you're not opposed to adopting children, right?"

Jill felt a glimmer of hope of saving this relationship. "Right! If I decide that I *need* children in my life, I can just adopt some."

Then she changed the subject, wanting to end the conversation and head home before saying something she might regret.

Book club questions for discussion.   *Chapters 1-12*

❖ *Secrets have a way of convicting a person with wrong desires and actions. What was Jill's secret in Chapter 1?*

❖ *At what time in a relationship should you talk about your thoughts and desires of having children in your future?*

❖ *What do you think Jill was hoping for when she said she hoped falling in love with the right man would change her desire about not having children?*

❖ *In Chapter 2, why do you think Jill didn't want to "defend" herself to remain childless? Do you think it was to avoid conviction or embarrassment of her reasoning?*

❖ *Do you think her convicted feelings are from God?*

❖ *In Chapter 3, what do you think Jill was hoping to hear from Brad when she asked him the hypothetical question?*

❖ *Do you agree with Brad that the reasons she doesn't want to have children are shallow and selfish?*

Book club questions for discussion.   *Chapters 1-12*

❖   *Do you think having children is more than having a maternal desire or the process of childbirth? Please list other reasons you should consider before having a child.*

❖   *In Jill's situation, why do you think she can't think on a deeper level and get past the child birthing?*

❖   *Do you think a long distance relationship can hinder or strengthen a relationship?*

❖   *Do you think Jill uses Brad's friendship more like a "boyfriend" due to the fact that Travis lives two and half hours away?*

❖   *What is your opinion about someone not wanting to physically have children, but to have them in their life through another source, as mentioned in Chapter 12?*

Chapter 13

The next morning Travis woke with the life drained out of him, taken aback by what Jill had said the previous night. He rolled over and looked at the clock, knowing he had to get up and hit the shower if he was going to make his flight to Tennessee. Jonah would be picking him up in less than a half hour to drop him off at the airport.

***

Travis's mother had a Matthew West song playing on the radio when Bo, her husband, walked into the kitchen.

"Mmm, something smells good!"

"Yes indeed, it's homemade mush," Bobby Sue replied, "along with some turkey bacon. You can either have a bowl of hot mush or I can fry some up for you."

Bo agreed to a bowl of hot mush, toast drizzled with cinnamon and honey, turkey bacon, and a cup of hot vanilla chai. The two of them loved breakfast time together when they could eat, pray, and share with one another.

As they finished breakfast, Bobby Sue cleared her throat. "Did you happen to see Travis this morning before he left for the airport?"

Bo looked up at his wife as he set down his cup. "No, but I did hear Jonah pull up early this morning in that jalopy he drives. Why?"

Bobby Sue looked concerned. "Well, I could tell when he came in last night that something wasn't right. When I asked him about it he said during his conversation with Jill she told him that she had no desire to have children."

Bo's eyes grew wide, then he wrinkled his forehead in disbelief. "What! Was she serious?"

Bobby Sue sighed and nodded. "I'm afraid she is."

Bo sat back in his chair with a heavy heart. "Oh man. You know how much Travis loves kids."

Bobby Sue slowly nodded. "Yes I do. I mean, that's one of the reasons he's so passionate about his doll line. He's all about kids. Jill is a wonderful Christian girl whom I adore, and I think that if it worked out, they could make beautiful babies."

Bo half grinned while he reached for Bobby Sue's hands. "Let's take this to the Lord."

"*Dear heavenly Father, we ask for You to be with Travis and Jill as they take a deeper look into their future. Whether they stay together and work something out or You have other plans for their future, please, Lord, give them understanding and discernment regarding the question of life partners. Please continue to shape and mold Travis's as well as our daughter Greta's life partner. You know the plans for their future. Let Travis, Jill, and Greta rely on Your guidance for their future partners. And as always, Lord, help Bobby Sue and me be Your light today. Let us shine for You and do Your will. In Jesus' name, amen.*"

Bobby Sue reached over and gently kissed Bo on the cheek. "Thanks."

Chapter 14

Jill woke recalling every word of her conversation she had with Travis the night before. In her heart she knew that he was the one for her, but as she lay in bed she wonder if something was wrong with her. *Why do people think it's so bad to not want to have children? Does it make me selfish that I don't want the pain and the changes my body will go through? What if I can't lose the weight afterwards? Will I still be attractive? Or is it that I'm aware of how many unwanted kids there are and want to know why should I bring another one into this world? I mean, if I want a child, I can just adopt one, right?*

Emotionally exhausted from the previous night, she didn't want to spend any more time to analyze it. She hopped out of bed and walked to the closet to choose an outfit that would work for classes and the first day at her new job. She was scheduled to work two hours after her last class. Wanting to look businesslike, she chose black slacks and a gray tunic sweater with a pink and gray floral scarf. She pulled her hair to one side in a long braid and accented it with a barrette on the other side of her part.

Tara ran into Jill's bedroom as Jill grabbed her make-up kit.

"Jill, you should have heard Brad and me sing at practice! Mr. Hook was really pleased." Tara started to dance around the room singing, "People Will Say We're in Love." Then she plopped face down on Jill's bed and looked over at her. "Well, one of us is in love."

Jill chuckled. "Oh Tara, if it's meant to be, it will be. Speaking of Brad, I wonder what hours he works today. Maybe I can catch a ride home from work with him."

Tara sat up on Jill's bed. "Jill, how do you see Brad?"

Jill looked at Tara's reflection in her make-up mirror. "What do you mean, how do I see him?"

"You know, like a brother, a friend, or some guy you could see yourself with long-term. I mean if Travis wasn't in the picture?"

Jill turned around and stared at Tara in disbelief. "Tara, do you think I'm interested in Brad as a boyfriend?"

"No!" Tara nervously fiddled with her bracelet. "Well, it just seems like he would do anything you ask him to do, no matter what. So—I don't know, I just want to know how you feel about him."

"Tara, my heart belongs to Travis. Brad is and always will be my friend. We grew up together. Our mothers are best friends. So it feels natural to do things with him, that's all."

Tara looked down at her hands and said in a low voice, "O—kay."

Chapter 15

Travis landed in Tennessee at ten o'clock that morning and looked for someone holding a sign with his name. After many conversations over the phone, Gary, the CEO of the doll trade show, appeared to be intrigued with Travis. He had instructed Sabrina, his daughter and assistant—a new graduate with a degree in business—to pick Travis up from the airport, and had scheduled a brunch for them once he landed.

Travis immediately spotted the tall, slender, strawberry blonde young woman, then noticed the sign she held with his name on it. He walked over and reached out to shake her hand. Appearing a little flustered, she dropped the sign in her effort to shake hands. When they both bent to retrieve it, they bumped heads.

Sabrina giggled. "I'm so sorry! I am used to picking up older clients for my dad, and it's refreshing to pick up someone my age who is interested in the same industry as we are."

With genuine joy, Travis smiled. "So you're Gary's daughter and business partner?"

"Yes, I'm Sabrina and I'll sit in on the brunch/meeting today. As a matter of fact, I'll be the one to drive you there now. Do you have any luggage you need to pick up?"

"Yes, I do."

After they claimed his luggage, they headed for the parking lot, discussing the trade show. When they got into Sabrina's copper Corvette she looked over at Travis. "So what's with this idea of a runway show?" She asked.

Travis, wanting to talk about her car instead, looked over at her. "Well, let's hold that conversation until we meet with your dad."

As Sabrina effortlessly zipped her Corvette in and out of airport traffic, he continued, "I want to know: does this have a stock engine or did you modify it?"

Sabrina laughed. "Well...maybe she's had some modifications done. Why?"

"Well, I'm impressed. By the way you just pulled away from that Camaro, it's clear that it's no longer a stock engine."

Sabrina had a winning smile, charming freckles generously sprinkled across her nose, and seemed truly comfortable with Travis. Her short sassy hair, framed by long bangs, blew in the wind as they pulled up to the cafe.

Her smile grew wider as she parked in front of the cafe and waved at her father who was already seated at an outdoor table. "Here we are, right on time. Daddy likes things done in a timely fashion."

Travis grabbed his briefcase and spoke softly, "So that's your excuse for the way you drive?"

Sabrina put her index finger up to her glossy pink lips. "Shh. Let's let this be our little secret, okay?"

Travis winked at her and suddenly felt energized after what had occurred the previous night, like a new beginning.

The meeting went well. Gary agreed to let Travis build a runway platform next to his booth. To have a live doll show would be a brand new attraction at the trade show. He appointed Sabrina to work with Travis on the color schemes for the runway platform and to coordinate it with the trade show color palette.

After their lunch, Travis and Sabrina went to a local fabric warehouse to pick out swatches of fabric for the curtains and skirting. From there, Sabrina drove toward her homestead where Gary had arranged for Travis to stay as their guest in the poolside guesthouse. She looked over at Travis. "Did you bring your swim trunks?"

He glanced back at her. "Did I hear you right? Did I bring swim trunks— to a business meeting?"

Sabrina laughed into the wind with the Corvette's top down. "You heard right. Did you?"

"No, was I supposed to?"

"Well, it's Indian summer here and because it might be the last of our good weather I've invited a few of my friends over for a cookout and a swim tonight. You're welcome to join us if you like."

"Well, considering I didn't bring my trunks, I'll have to pass."

Sabrina whipped her 'Vette into the next turn lane. "Oh, no worries. We can buy some."

The next thing Travis knew he was in the swimwear section of a department store.

"Here, try these on." Sabrina picked up a pair of trunks. "You look like a medium."

Travis grabbed the swim trunks from her. As he headed to the dressing room, he heard her say, "Oh, and yeah. I want to see how they fit." He shook his head in disbelief, wondering how he'd gotten himself roped into modeling swimwear.

"Travis? Come on out, I want to see how they fit."

When Travis came out of the dressing room, he still had his business shirt and tie on, along with his dress socks.

Sabrina giggled as she pointed her finger at him. "Stay right there." She ran over to a rack of tee shirts and grabbed one that would match the swim trunks. "Here, put this on with the swim trunks and take your socks off. I can't introduce you to my friends wearing swim trunks with a business shirt, tie, and socks!"

By the time they left the store, Sabrina had color coordinated a beach towel, flip flops, and sunglasses to go with the swim trunks, putting them on her father's credit card as a business expense.

Chapter 16

Brad read Tara's text as he sat in his car after work. "Did you get the text? Mr. Hook is calling for a full cast meeting tonight. Hannah broke her ankle cheering at Friday night's football game. He wants to work up a schedule for all cast members who have a part with the two of us. The show is in a couple of weeks and he wants to give me plenty of rehearsal time."

Brad texted her back. "Yeah, I'm waiting on Jill to get off work, so if you like, I can pick you up when I drop her off and we can ride together. What time did he want to meet?"

"In two hours," Tara replied.

"Okay, c u then."

***

Jill high-stepped it out of the building toward Brad's car once he tooted the horn. "Hey, you look like an easy pick-up," he teased.

Jill grinned as she jumped into his car. "I'm starved! Do you have time to go eat somewhere?"

"Yes, as a matter of fact I don't have to be anywhere for a couple of hours. Where do you want to go?"

"Anywhere we can sit outside and eat. I love this warm breeze." Jill shifted in her seat to look at him. "Brad, I really think my bosses liked me today!"

"Really? What makes you say that?"

"Well, I got to go into the warehouse and meet the people on the production line. Hey, I thought you started working today. But I didn't see you in there."

"I had some paperwork to sign today. I must have been in the warehouse office when you were on your tour."

"That makes sense. Well, as I said, everyone there smiled at me and made me feel welcome."

With a half grin on his face, Brad tilted his head toward her. "I'm not surprised, Jill, because most of the warehouse workers are men. And…well, you're not hard to look at."

"Oh, Brad!" Jill slapped his arm. "It's not just about looks, you know. It's about my personality, too."

Brad pulled into the local Ma and Pa diner which offered table service on the patio. Indian summer was in the air. The waitress took their order and offered them some popcorn while they waited for their food. As she walked away, Brad pulled out his phone to check his emails. While he did that, Jill called Travis to see how his meeting went with Gary.

Chapter 17

Travis—enjoying Sabrina's cookout in his new swim attire—felt his phone vibrate in his pocket. He looked at it and saw Jill's name pop up. Immediately his emotions changed from upbeat to a weird sense of emptiness. He hurriedly walked toward the guesthouse, not far from the pool, wanting to answer before it went to voicemail.

"Hello?"

"Hey, Travis, it's me. How did your meeting go today?" Sabrina and her friends' loud laughter, with the deafening background music, made it hard for Travis to hear.

"Sorry. What did you say?"

Jill spoke louder. "Where are you? And what are you doing!?"

"Hey, can I call you later? I can't hear you very well."

With a huff from Jill she ended the call. She sat quietly as the waitress delivered their meals.

Brad set down his phone. "Is everything all right?"

Jill shrugged. Hesitantly, Brad asked if it was okay to pray over their dinner. Jill nodded as she sat up straighter and bowed her head, her hands folded around her phone.

Before Brad said amen, Jill added, "Dear Lord, please watch over Travis while he's on his business trip. And don't let this food turn into fat. Amen."

"Is everything all right between you and Travis?"

Jill looked down at her food and pushed it around on her plate. "Oh, I don't know—I just called and could hear nothing but laughter and loud music."

Brad swallowed a big gulp of his drink and said, "I heard you yell into the phone." He grabbed her hand and squeezed and then released it. "Listen, it's probably not a big deal. I'm sure he'll explain when he calls you back. You shouldn't waste your time fretting about it. If I'm not mistaken, you said you were starved, so why don't you eat? Hey! I'll even stop on the way home and get you a smoothie, okay?"

Jill smiled at his offer of a smoothie. "You always know what to say to cheer me up. Okay, you talked me into it. I'm not going to let it bother me. Besides, I prayed about it and now it's in the Lord's hands. I just hope Travis listens to Him."

***

Travis walked back toward the party as they talked about playing a game of "Chicken" in the pool. Sabrina yelled, "Travis is my partner!"

He frowned. "Wait, what?"

Sabrina explained how to play the game. "Everyone gets in the shallow part of the pool and each girl sits on top of her partner's shoulders. Then when the whistle blows they try to push the other team's girl off her partner's shoulders. The last couple standing wins."

Before Travis could gracefully refuse, Sabrina grabbed the phone from his hand and set it on the table. She took hold of his upper arm, slid down to his hand then ran, hand in hand, to the deep end of the pool. After gathering momentum, she leaped into the air and landed almost on top of him in the water.

Sabrina's head came up out of the water first and she yelled, "Woohoo! Let the games begin!" Travis emerged from the water, gasping for breath, struggling to keep the pace with Sabrina.

The next thing he heard from her was, "I'll race you to the shallow end." And off she went.

Travis couldn't resist, and yelled, "You win!"

She quickly responded with a splash and a kick of her legs.

Chapter 18

Tara waited at her bedroom window where she could watch for Brad's car. As she looked at her reflection in the window, she wondered, *What's he doing with Jill? It's been an hour and a half since I texted him. Surely Jill didn't work overtime on her first day of work. I know she's an overachiever, but really, on her first day?* Then she comforted herself. *He'll be here soon enough. Just be patient.* She turned to look at the time and then back out the window. Finally, she saw his car turn onto their street and her heart began to race.

Jill grabbed the door handle as she looked over to Brad, thanked him for the ride and for hanging out with her. "It would have been a long night alone and going crazy with thoughts about what Travis was doing tonight."

Brad patted her knee. "Any time, Jill, any time."

Just then Tara ran down the stairs and out to Brad's car. "Hi, Jill."

Jill looked surprised when she got out of the car. "Well, hey—what's going on?"

"Oh, didn't Brad tell you that he's giving me a ride to play practice?"

"No, I guess he's a man of few words. Well, have fun and I'll see you when you get home."

Jill smiled as she waved at Brad. "Thanks again."

"Yeah, sure, no problem. I hope your talk goes well with Travis tonight."

"Me too." She smiled at Tara, whose grin was ear to ear.

***

Travis didn't call Jill back until eleven-thirty Nashville time which made it ten-thirty in Ohio. He really wasn't in the mood to talk to her after his enjoyable evening with Sabrina and her friends. He leaned back against the headboard of his bed and looked through the pictures stored on his phone. Sabrina's friend had grabbed it off the table and had taken pictures during the chicken fight and, of course, captured some of the winning team. Sabrina had just about drowned him as she fought for the championship. But he wasn't sure how much of that he wanted to share with Jill.

She answered her phone on the first ring. "Travis?"

"Hey there. Are you still up?"

"Yes! What did you think? That I wouldn't want to talk to you after you couldn't hear me when I called you hours ago?"

Oh boy, this is not going to go well.

"Where were you and what were you doing?"

Travis cleared his throat. "Well, I'm staying at Gary's estate as a guest. They had a cookout with some friends and invited me to join them. That's where I was when you called."

"All night? You couldn't have called me back sooner? What were you doing all that time?" Travis hesitated. He knew it wouldn't be a good idea to go into detail.

He cut to the chase. "Would you like to hear about the meeting, or did you just call to check up on me earlier?"

She could tell by the tone in his voice that she should let it rest. "Tell me about the meeting."

She became quiet, however, when he told her about Sabrina taking him to get swatches of fabric for the runway stage.

"But I told you that I wanted to do that."

"Jill, Gary suggested it because Sabrina knows the trade show's color schemes. She's his partner in the business, and he feels this is a part of her job description."

She waited a few seconds then responded, "Who is this Sabrina anyway, and how old is she?"

Travis rubbed his temples. "As I already said, she's Gary's daughter and also his business partner."

"What does she look like? Is she married?"

"Jill, stop! It's late and I have an early flight back tomorrow. We can continue this conversation tomorrow."

She didn't want to end the conversation, but she knew she had no other choice. "Goodnight, Travis. I can't wait to talk to you tomorrow."

Travis suggested that she try to relax and get a good night's sleep. Then he pressed *end call* and flipped back over to his pictures...to look at something pleasant—Sabrina.

***

The next morning Travis woke to the sound of an alarm. It wasn't any ordinary alarm, but Sabrina, who burst into the guesthouse, and rambled on about how he needed to get up if he wanted breakfast by the pool.

"It's a beautiful Tennessee morning!" she said, then continued, "We need to make the most of your new swimwear and swim a couple laps in the pool before we head to the airport."

In disbelief, Travis thought he was still dreaming. *Is she really standing over me...while I'm in bed?*

She had picked up his swim trunks from the back of a chair and tossed them at him. He grabbed the trunks off of his head where they landed.

"Whoa, how did you get in here? And what time is it?"

It was an awkward moment when Sabrina reached over to pull him up. "Come on, get up. We gotta make the most of the time you have here." Without warning she flipped his covers back and grabbed his legs to swing them over the edge of the bed, making him glad he wore pajamas to bed.

His head was spinning. That's what Sabrina was good at, making his head spin.

"Wait! You didn't answer my question. How did you get in here?"

Sabrina smiled. "Oh, you know…I have my own key."

"Of course you do."

***

On the flight home Travis wondered when he would see Sabrina again. He looked through his briefcase and saw the sample fabrics she had picked out for the runway platform and pondered, *I wonder if Jill will like these?*

He rested his head against the headrest and thought back to the conversation with Jill about children. Still in disbelief, he couldn't get past her statement that if she needed a child, she would just adopt. *Should I continue to put time into this relationship or should I end it?*

He closed his briefcase and looked out the window. When the plane started to descend, he realized he was almost home.

Chapter 19

Tara couldn't stifle her excitement no matter how hard she tried. She loved the fact that she and Brad were now pretty much inseparable, because of all the play practice. The homecoming dance was two weeks away and she was hopeful. She had never been asked to a school dance by a guy, let alone Homecoming.

Jill was cleaning in the kitchen when Tara bounced in. "Hi, Tara. Who ya thinkin' about with that smile on your face?"

Tara reached for an apple off the counter. "One guess."

Jill laughed. "Um, Brad? The one and only, your McDreamy."

Tara sighed aloud. "Jill, are you going to ask Travis to Homecoming?"

Jill—who felt Travis was a little distant since she'd admitted her true feelings about children, was hesitant with her reply. "Well, I would love for him to take me. Why do you ask? Are you going to ask Brad?"

Tara immediately blushed. "Oh, I would love it if he asked me. After all, we have spent most of our evenings together with all the play rehearsals." She pulled out a chair and sat down at the kitchen table. "Jill, can I share something with you?"

Jill put the washcloth down and settled into the chair beside Tara. She could hear a little sadness in her friend's voice. "Sure. What is it?"

"Well, I've never been asked to a school dance. Okay, let me say that the one time I did get asked, he canceled the week of the dance."

Jill gasped. "What? Who would do that?"

Tara nodded. "Exactly! His excuse was that he felt sorry for this girl from his school. She was a senior who didn't have a date and since I didn't go to his school, he thought I would understand if he took her instead."

Jill hit the table with her fist. "What a jerk!"

"I don't want to go through that kind of disappointment again."

Jill stared at nothing for a few seconds. "Tara, I wonder if you should ask a guy. It might make you feel more confident that he wouldn't do something like that to you."

Tara met her gaze. "So, do you think if I asked Brad that he would accept and follow through?"

"Mmm, Brad isn't much of a dancer, but I know that if he did accept, he wouldn't back out. So, are you going to ask him?"

Just then Jill's phone buzzed and she grabbed it off the kitchen counter. "Oh, it's Travis! I have to take this call."

"Yeah, sure, I understand. I'll talk to you later." Tara got up and left the room.

"Hi Travis, I'm so glad you called. It feels like forever since I've seen you!"

"Yes, it has been awhile. I've been extremely busy and it's not going to slow down anytime soon."

Jill was not happy with his response. "Oh really—what's going on?"

She heard Travis take a deep breath before he responded. "Well, after giving it a great deal of thought, I'm wondering if maybe we should take a break from our relationship. We don't see each other but once a month with you so far away at college and my increasingly busy schedule."

Jill's eyes instantly filled with tears and her voice trembled when she spoke. "What!? Are you breaking up with me over the phone?"

"Now Jill, don't look at it as a bad thing. I mean, think about it. This is your senior year of college and I'm so busy that I can no longer get to the school events the way a boyfriend should. So—I thought maybe we could take a break and see how we feel down the road."

"Travis! Let's hang up and face-time. I need to see you!"

Travis accepted Jill's call. He complimented her outfit but that didn't make her feel better.

"Look Travis, I don't want to break things off. I think if we really try to put down all our activities on a calendar we could make more of an effort to see each other. I can drive down on the weekends when you're not traveling and you can come up here for school events. Like Homecoming that's coming up shortly."

"But that's just it. I have to travel the next few weekends with this runway project."

She burst into tears and sobbed out loud.

"Listen Jill, I don't want you to miss out on the things you enjoy doing with your school. This is your senior year and I know how important those things are to you. I hate to keep on disappointing you when I can't be a part of it."

Jill tried to compose herself, blowing her nose and then using her fingertips to dry her eyes. "Could you at least come to Homecoming?"

"When is it?"

"It's two weeks from now."

Hesitantly, Travis answered, "I'm supposed to fly out to a doll show in Oklahoma that week, and I don't know how long I'll be there. Gary wants me to see this venue. It's one of the biggest events of the year. He thinks I need to talk to the local agencies who can supply us with models and hair stylists."

"Why?"

"To compare the cost of using hired models or bringing my own. If I do all my homework now, I should be ready for the show circuit next year."

Tears streamed down her cheeks. "Will you please try to make it?"

With a big sigh, he said, "I'll think about it, Jill, and we'll see how it goes. But, for now I want you to make plans to go. If someone asks you, then I want you to go with him. You deserve to go. It's your senior Homecoming. I don't want you to miss out because of me."

Jill held her head up with one hand, wiping her eyes with the other. "I have to go, Travis," she said. "I don't feel well."

"Okay. I'll talk to you later this week."

Jill turned off her phone, ran to her bedroom, crawled under the covers, and wept.

Chapter 20

It was Sunday morning and the girls had made plans to meet Brad and his roommates at the coffee shop before church. Jill was in a subdued mood; she had shared with her roommates some of the conversation she'd had with Travis.

The coffee shop was full of college students talking about the Homecoming theme. Tara began to review who would be going with whom. That was her subtle way of asking Brad if he would like to go with her. Better yet, to let him know that she didn't have a date so that maybe he would ask her.

"So, Jackie and Sadie, you guys are going as double dates with your boyfriends to Homecoming, correct?"

Jackie spoke up. "Yes, since our boyfriends are on the football team, we're actually going with some of the other football players and their dates."

"Oh, that makes sense," Then she looked over at Jill. "Have you asked Travis yet if he's able to go with you?"

Jill dreaded the question and wanted to avoid the answer as long as possible. Finally, she glanced from Tara to Brad and back again. "Better yet, Tara, have *you* asked anyone yet?"

Tara's neck turned red when her discomfort forced her to fall into character as Annie, from the play.

"Um, you know, if Curly is too busy I might ask Jed to Homecoming." Everyone at the table laughed, knowing the actor who played Jed had a girlfriend.

Sadie looked at Brad. "Well, Curly, are you going to leave Annie stranded, or are you going to ask her to Homecoming?"

Brad squirmed in his chair, and glanced over at Jill. "Well—um—is Travis coming up?"

Jill's stomach ached; she didn't want to talk about it anymore. All she wanted to do was to head over to church and hear some good preaching from Pastor Neil. Ignoring the question, she stood up and in an authoritative voice said, "Okay guys, we'd better head over to church. We don't want to be late."

Pastor Neil's sermon that morning was taken from Genesis 29 about Jacob and the two sisters. Jacob was a handsome guy who had an eye for Laban's beautiful younger daughter, Rachel. It was the custom for a man to offer a substantial gift to the family of his future wife for their daughter. Jacob agreed to work seven years in exchange for marriage to Rachel. When the seven years ended, Laban instead gave him the oldest daughter, Leah, telling Jacob that it was their custom to marry off the oldest daughter first. So, Jacob, who'd been tricked, married her and worked another seven years to marry Rachel.

Pastor Neil continued on with the story of the two women and how God showed favor to Leah, as she was not chosen by Jacob and felt unloved. In fact, God favored her with the ability to bear children and left Rachel barren. This, of course, made Rachel jealous, so she offered Jacob her maidservant so that she would bear a child for her and then she, too, would build a family for Jacob.

Jill felt convicted hearing this story, easily applying it to what was going on in her life.

Here's Tara, playing second fiddle to me whenever Brad is around, even though I don't have those kind of feelings for him. I know it bothers her that we're so close. Then knowing Travis wants a family, while I am electing, by my own desires, to not have any children. Am I trying to please Travis the way Rachel was trying to please Jacob, by telling him that I would consider adopting a child? Why am I thinking this way? Jill excused herself from the pew and headed straight for the bathroom.

After she lost her breakfast inside the stall, Jill wet some paper towels and held them to the back of her neck. This was the only way to calm herself. Finally, she heard the benediction and knew she had to pull herself together so her roommates wouldn't ask questions. Luckily no one was in the restroom so she took her ever-present toothbrush and toothpaste from her purse, brushed her teeth, and rinsed out her mouth.

As Jill walked out of the restroom, Tara met her. "Are you okay? You've been quiet all morning."

Jill replied, "I'm okay. It's just that breakfast didn't agree with me."

When Brad looked at her intently she nodded with a half-smile and mouthed the words, "I'm okay."

It was still Indian summer weather as they exited the church so Brad asked if anyone was up for Ultimate Frisbee at the park.

Tara was the first to respond. "I am!"

Brad looked over at Jill. "Are you up for a game?"

Jill smiled and shrugged her shoulders, then said, "What's in it for the winning team?"

"Oh, I don't know. What do you think the prize should be?"

"Well, it depends on who's on my team."

"Why would that matter?"

"Well, because if you're on my team we would for sure lose, and I don't like losing."

Brad shook his head. "What? Oh, Jill, that's it. I'm not going to be on your team, and your team is going down! I don't care if you have the whole football team on your side. You are going down!"

Jill said confidently, "Bring it on! I'll be at the park by two o'clock with my team. Be ready to be my slave for a day, Bradley, because this girls' team is going to win!"

Chapter 21

Jill walked through the house with little hope that Travis would make it to Homecoming. Her roomies buzzed around her in a last-minute preparation to get out the door. Sadie and Jackie had to leave early to have pictures taken on the football field with their boyfriends. Tara and Jill were going over to Brad's place as he and one of his roommates, Tim, were going together. No one ever mentioned who was going with whom. A few of Tim's friends from the tennis team were going to meet them at the school dance. Jill held onto the hope that Travis would make it back from Oklahoma in time to take her.

Tara looked beautiful in her Homecoming dress—fitted, long, and royal blue with the top tailored to hang off the edge of her shoulders. She had her hair pulled up in a twisted braid with a few wisps of hair framing her face.

Jill's choice was a short cocktail dress of black satin, decked out in pearl accessories. She straightened her long curly hair and added sprigs of baby's breath just the way Travis liked it. She tried to stay upbeat and happy about this evening as she remembered Tara's story. Deep in her heart she longed for Travis to be with her. He had given her very little hope that he would make it, but she just couldn't let go of the want.

"Tara, are you ready to go?"

Tara was already perspiring with nerves. "As ready as I'll ever be."

As they drove over to Brad and Tim's place, Tara spoke first. "Jill, I know you're sad that Travis is unable to take you tonight, but look at this dance as if you had never met him, and make the most of our last Homecoming dance. After all, you said you guys have pretty much broken up."

Jill gave her a sad smile. "You're right and I'm really going to try to have fun. After all, I have the best date with me right now. I can't wait to see you dance with Brad tonight."

"Oh, I hope he asks me!"

After arriving at the guys' house, they sat in the car and made a pact that no matter what, they were going to have the time of their lives. No man was going to ruin it for them. They hooked their pinky fingers together and counted to three. In an upward motion they lifted their hands up as they opened up their fingers in an explosive way to the sky and both shouted, "Let's do this!"

On the front porch they composed themselves before Tim finally opened the door.

"Whoa, you two look amazing! Come on in." He yelled up the stairs as he walked behind them, "Hey, Brad, the girls are here." Walking to the kitchen, he asked, "Do you girls want something to drink?"

Tara replied, "Yes, please. I'll take some water."

Jill nodded. "That sounds good. I'll have mine with ice, please."

As Brad strolled into the room in a black tux, Tara stood motionless, the glass still at her mouth. "Whoa!" Tara blew out a breath making bubble sounds in her water. Once she realized what she had done, she inhaled more water, tilted her glass down, and started to cough.

Brad hurried to her side and patted her back. "Tara, are you okay?" He reached for her glass and set it down on the side table.

Tara, completely embarrassed, felt her face redden, as she continued to cough.

"Excuse me." She ran to the bathroom, shut the door, and leaned against it.

Jill ran after her. "Tara, are you okay? Let me in."

Tara rolled her body off of the bathroom door and opened the door.

As soon as Jill saw that Tara was okay, she said, "Well, there's the real reason they didn't name you Grace!" They both burst into laughter.

Chapter 22

While Travis was en route to the Oklahoma airport from the toy trade show, he thought about the homecoming dance that evening. Looking at his watch, he calculated the time when the plane would land, then realized he would have time to go home, clean up, and drive to Canton in time to have the last dance with Jill. He knew how much it would mean to her and for that reason wanted to make it happen. But deep down he felt confused, especially after Sabrina made it clear that she was interested in him as more than a business associate.

Travis, just do it! You can get there before the dance is over. It will mean the world to Jill. It will relieve some of the guilt you feel about pulling away from her since she revealed her feelings about having children. He got on his phone, texted his mom, told her of his plans and asked if she could have his tux ready and cut some flowers from her garden. Bobby Sue was happy to help out. Travis put his phone away and was excited about surprising Jill.

***

Brad walked around the car to open the door for Jill and Tara. Tim saw the tennis team gathered in a circle outside the building and looked back at Brad and the girls. "Hey, guys, I'll meet you inside. I'm going to go over and talk to some friends of mine."

They acknowledged him, and headed toward the school doors.

Inside, they were amazed with the dramatic change in the appearance of the room. Silver and gold foil decorations spiraled down from the ceiling, and dimmed lights lit the dance floor as the fog floated over the floor in an invitation to dance, while soft rock music played in the background. Round tables were set up all around the dance floor, and against the walls were tables lined with finger foods and punch bowls. In the hallway near the restrooms was a table with long stemmed roses for sale. The air was filled with the mingled scents of flowers, food items and favorite fragrances.

Brad led the girls to tables at the far left corner of the dance floor where Tim and his friends met them. Tara and Jill began the evening by line dancing together. Toward the end of the night the DJ changed it up to slow songs. That's when they grabbed some punch and headed back to their table.

Jill saw Brad in conversation with some cast members at the back wall. She caught his attention and motioned for him to dance with Tara. Momentarily he walked over and whispered in Tara's ear. She nodded, and the two began to dance. As they left, Jill grabbed her phone and took pictures of them. She was thrilled for her, like a proud mom watching a daughter's first dance.

A few guys asked Jill to dance but she politely declined since her heart belonged to Travis.

When the song ended the DJ invited everyone onto the dance floor; it was time to announce the Homecoming king and queen. As the girls predicted, the cheerleader with the broken leg was voted queen and the quarterback was voted king. The DJ then asked everyone to pick a partner for the last slow dance of the night.

As Tara and Jill headed back toward their table, Tara turned to Jill. "I want you to dance with Brad. It's the last dance of the night."

Jill smiled. "Tara, baby, this is your homecoming—your night, and he's your knight in shining armor. You dance with him."

They were scanning the room for Brad when he walked toward them with a rose in his hand.

Suddenly Jill gasped, covered her mouth with her hands and burst into tears. There he was: Travis in a black tux, carrying a bouquet of wildflowers. Jill sprinted toward him and threw her arms around his waist.

He held out the flowers with one hand and hugged her with the other. "Jill, may I have this dance?"

Jill nodded as she held him tightly.

He chuckled. "Hey, we're gonna miss the dance. Let's go show them how it's done."

Jill giggled. "Yes, let's do it."

As they danced to the song, "My Eyes Adore You," Brad walked over to Tara, handed her the long-stemmed red rose and lead her onto the dance floor. This was a night both she and Jill would cherish forever.

The four of them danced until the DJ announced that the photo booth would close in fifteen minutes.

Jill looked at Travis. "We have to get pictures to memorialize the night!"

Jill nodded for Brad and Tara to follow her and Travis. Walking off the dance floor, Tara asked Jill, "Where are we going?"

Jill looked at her. "Didn't you hear the DJ? The photo booth will close soon, so we need to get pictures taken."

"Oh, you're not kidding." Tara grabbed Brad's hand and pulled him toward the booth. After a short discussion they decided they would all get in together, where they took four photo shots. Tara's favorite was the one where she sat on the stool and Brad faced her with open arms and a rose between his teeth. She had her hands cupped around her face, while Jill and Travis stood behind them with Jill's wildflowers held high, like a victory trophy.

In Jill's favorite she sat lengthwise across Travis's lap with her legs crossed at the ankles, while she leaned back against him with her arms stretched up high. Travis held the bouquet of flowers in his right hand at her waist. Brad and Tara stood over them with their arms arched in a heart shape over them. When they were done, they headed back to their table, amused with their pictures.

***

The girls went to the restroom as the guys took seats at the table. Brad let out a long breath as he loosened his tie. "What a night. Hey, Travis, I'm surprised to see you here!"

"Yeah, I wasn't too sure I would make it. Do you think I can crash at your place tonight?"

"Sure, you know you're always welcome anytime you need a place to stay."

Travis extended his hand to shake on it. "Thanks Brad, I really appreciate it. How's school going?"

"Good. I'll be glad to graduate and work with my hands again."

"Aw, that's right. You're going to graduate with a construction engineering degree, correct?"

"Yes, I want to be active in construction, and not only the engineering part. I want to…."

Jill and Tara sat down at the table and she interrupted, "I'm ready to leave whenever you are, Travis. We have so much to catch up on. I thought we could go back to my place for a while."

Everyone nodded in agreement. Brad stood, looked over at Tara, and said he wanted to go find Tim before they headed back to his house. Tara offered to go with him.

Chapter 23

Travis opened the Jeep door for Jill. She giggled a little as she hopped in. "I can't believe you brought the Jeep! I'm glad we're leaving early so no one sees me leave a formal dance in a Jeep." However, she was so happy that Travis had made it to the dance that she didn't make too big of a deal over the vehicle he took her home in.

"Just think of it as a great conversation piece."

Jackie and Sadie were still out with their dates when Jill and Travis pulled up to the house. They decided to sit on the porch swing in the Indian summer breeze.

Jill spoke first. "You don't know how much it means to me that you came tonight!"

He put his arm around her shoulders, and pulled her closer then kissed the top of her head. "I know it does. I'm glad I could make it."

They sat in silence for a few minutes before Jill brought up their relationship. "Travis, I know we talked about taking a break from our relationship, but I wonder if you'd consider staying together until after I graduate."

Travis sat in quiet contemplation before he finally answered. "How do you think that would change our relationship?"

"Well, I think once I graduate and move closer to you, we'd have more time to see each other on a regular basis. Then if we—well, if you still feel the same way, we can go our own separate ways. I think long distance dating has been our problem."

"Would that change the way you feel about having children?"

She looked down at her hands and then back at Travis. "Right now I'd have to say no. But—who knows how we'll feel once we actually have a normal relationship—spending more time together?"

They sat in silence, rocking on the porch swing, before he finally answered, "Okay, let's see how we feel once you graduate and move back home."

Jill excitedly wrapped her arms around his neck in a big squeeze. "Oh thank you. This has been an amazing night! One I will never forget. I love you!"

"I love you too."

Chapter 24

Bo and Bobby Sue walked hand in hand up the hill to the old farmhouse. Bobby Sue's parents, Clara and Joe, had lived in it since they were married and had raised Bobby Sue there, even after turning the place into a bed & breakfast. After she married Bo, they built a second house for their family on another part of the property. Bobby Sue grew up as an only child, but she never felt like one because not only did she enjoy the company of her big extended family, but all the guests at the bed & breakfast.

Her mother had always loved children and was involved with kids in need. That's where Bobby Sue got her passion for orphans.

Bo and Bobby Sue walked into the foyer with the original oak floor and a beautiful circular staircase that wound up to the second floor. The welcome counter was placed to the right of the foyer, near the room that used to be the "pastor's room." It was always kept presentable in case the pastor stopped by to visit the family. Later on it turned into a small gift shop during the years of the bed and breakfast, offering homemade soaps, candles and quilts. The baked goods, jellies, and seasonal garden items were also always irresistible to the guests. Bobby Sue's father was a skilled woodworker, making birdhouses, small stools, porch swings, child-size stilts, and he enjoyed whittling birds and other animals to sell.

Since today was her parents' sixtieth wedding anniversary, Bobby Sue thought it would be nice to make them breakfast. They walked farther into the house to the room called the "Grand Room" where people held wedding receptions and large parties. Bobby Sue couldn't help fondly remembering all the incredible celebrations held there.

Without warning she said, "Oh, Bo, I was wondering—what would you think of reopening the B&B?"

Bo smiled. "Are you serious?"

"I am. I really miss it. We could even…" she continued as she looked around "…offer the Grand Room to Jill's parents for her graduation party. And we could celebrate Thanksgiving up here, too."

Bo was just about to say something when she continued, "Once we meet the current county building codes we could advertise it for weddings, receptions, conference meetings, and other parties. Let's rebirth this place! What do you think?"

"Well, it would need a lot of work to meet the codes."

"Yes, it would, but Travis and Greta could help, and it would give Mom and Dad a way to make new memories with the kids. They could also help groom the staff once it's ready. I hate to see the family business fade away along with this house. It still has a lot to give."

Bo smiled from ear to ear. "I like the way you think! It's a great idea. Let's go see if they agree."

***

Clara and Joe loved to start the day with cookies and coffee.

"Hi, Mom. Hi, Dad! We came to make you breakfast for your anniversary!"

Her parents looked up from the TV, surprised to see them.

Clara spoke up first. "Oh, how wonderful!"

Joe's face lit up. "Well, there she is!"

"Yep, it's me! Are you ready for a healthy home-cooked breakfast?"

Clara turned the TV down and said, "Well, we already had our cookies and coffee. Can you sit down awhile and visit before you start cooking?"

Bo lifted up the bags in his hands and said, "Let me drop these groceries off in the kitchen."

Joe looked over and grinned at Bobby Sue. "So, what do you know?"

Bobby Sue pulled out a chair from the table as she thought, *Wow, Lord, you made this convenient.*

"Well, Dad, I was just thinking about this place and wondered what you and Mom would think if we decided to turn it back into a bed and breakfast again. I mean you guys would still have your own private area and you wouldn't have to run it unless you wanted to."

They both chuckled as Joe spoke first. "I can tell you right now that we'd rather not run it. But what made you think to open it up again?"

Bo walked back into the room and chuckled. "That's a loaded question."

"There are lots of reasons," Bobby Sue answered. "It's a beautiful place that sits in a beautiful setting and I couldn't help remembering all the good times people have had here. Plus, it would give you guys some company. You wouldn't have to do a thing, except monitor what we're doing, and give advice on how to do things. I hate to see all your experience and talents go to waste. You can teach the next generation a lot with all your wisdom."

Clara smiled as she leaned toward Joe. "Boy, she sure knows how to make it sound good."

They continued to talk over the details and reminisced about the "good ol' days" until they discovered they were hungry and decided to turn breakfast into brunch.

Chapter 25

All week Tara was in a dream state after her night at Homecoming. With a full dress rehearsal scheduled in a few hours, she knew she had to focus on being ready. The show would be opening in two days. She hadn't seen Brad since the dance and wasn't sure how he felt about their relationship, so she was thrilled when he texted her and offered to pick her up. She saw it as a good sign.

Just then Jill knocked on Tara's bedroom door.

"May I come in?"

Tara jumped off the bed and opened the door. "Yeah, sure, what's up?"

Jill did a little dance then she grabbed the bedpost and sat down on the bed. "I wanted to tell you that Travis and I are back together!"

"What! That's great! I mean I wasn't even sure you'd really broken up."

Jill beamed. "I know, we kinda talked about taking a break before Homecoming but we've decided to stay together. I'm excited to be able to spend Thanksgiving with his family. Then I'll head off to New York for the fashion show after which Travis and I will visit New York for a day and fly home together."

"Wow, it sounds like you have it all planned. So does that mean you won't be able to come to the musical this weekend?"

"I wish I could, but this will be my first holiday with Travis and his family."

Tara walked over to the window to watch for Brad's car and felt both relieved and excited for Jill.

"If I were in your shoes, I would miss the musical too. Any minute now Brad should be pulling up to the house. Hey, do you think Brad sees us as a couple now?"

"I don't know. Did he say anything after Homecoming that would lead you to believe that?"

Tara looked down and hesitantly said. "Um, no—not really. But Jill, it was so magical when we danced! And he did give me a rose!"

Jill nodded. "Yes! He sure did. So, I don't know, maybe he's falling for you now that you've spent so much time rehearsing together."

Tara looked up with hope and, as she did, she saw his car turn onto their road. "Um, he's here! I gotta go. Wish me luck that he asks me to be his girl!"

"Luck, Tara baby!"

Tara waved at her.

Brad yelled out the car window, "Is Jill home?"

Tara's hopeful mood dropped like a falling stone. *"Why does he want to know if Jill is home?"* She spoke up louder so he could hear her. "Um—Yeah, she's upstairs. Why?"

Brad opened his door and added, "Well, I wanted to see if she wanted to watch the dress rehearsal."

Tara stopped in her tracks. "I can run back in and ask her." She turned back toward the house, and grumbled loud enough for her ears only, "Tara, you have got to stop feeling insecure every time he talks about Jill. She's back with Travis so there's nothing to worry about."

Once Jill slid into the car with Tara and Brad, Tara looked over at Brad and broke the news.

"So, Brad, have you heard that Travis and Jill are closer than ever?"

Knowing that there was some turmoil between Jill and Travis, Brad looked into the rearview mirror to see Jill's expression. "Is that so? Well, good for you, Jill."

She beamed. "Yep, we're back on track!"

Tara was glad Brad knew about Jill and Travis. Now maybe he would give her his full attention.

***

Jill was amazed with the Oklahoma musical. Tara and Brad were very convincing, making spectators believe they were as in love as Curly and Annie by the way they gazed into each other's eyes. There was a tug at her heart as she sat there during the rehearsal. The one thing that still stood between Travis and her was the difference of opinion regarding children. She wondered if she would ever change her mind about that. How far would she go to hold onto Travis? Would she promise to have at least one child to hold onto him? Would she keep her promise? Oh, she didn't like that inner voice echoing through her mind. Jill suddenly felt overly warm and noticed her heart had started to beat faster as her anxiety rose. Quickly, she started to repeat Philippians 4:6 and 7 under her breath: *Do not be anxious about anything, but in everything, by prayer and petition with thanksgiving present your requests to God. And the peace of God which transcends all understanding will guard your hearts and your minds in Christ Jesus.* She blew out a deep breath and thought, *Okay, I'm giving it to You. God. You know my future.*

When the rehearsal was over, the audience gave the cast a standing ovation, and Jill applauded with the rest. She was happy that Brad had asked her to come to rehearsal. With her plans to share Thanksgiving weekend with Travis and his family, she was grateful for the opportunity to see her friends in the musical.

Chapter 26

Jill was excited to pack her weekend bag. She couldn't wait to get to Travis's house for Thanksgiving. Her parents had made travel plans to visit their other daughter, Shannon, and their first granddaughter, Ellie. Shannon's husband, Jarmar, was deployed, which left Shannon alone for the Thanksgiving holiday.

***

Bo walked into Travis's bedroom. "Hey, are you going on the annual pheasant and rabbit hunt in the morning with your grandpa and me?"

Travis nodded slowly. "Yes, what time?"

As they talked over the specific time, location, weapons, and ammo they would use, Travis's phone jingled. He glanced over and saw he had a text. He quickly swiped open the screen with his finger and saw that it was from Sabrina.

"Hey, cowboy! I've been thinking about you and wanted to wish you a Happy Thanksgiving! I miss seeing you in those swim trunks you modeled for me! Ha ha! Shirt, tie, and all! I look forward to working with you next year! With lots of love, your Champion Girl."

Travis grinned as he turned off his phone. He thought back to when he first met Sabrina at the airport, driving around in her sports car, modeling swimwear, and winning the chicken fight.

Still grinning, he felt an unfamiliar emotion surface as he thought about how Sabrina letting herself into the guest house to wake him up, hosting breakfast by the pool, and especially when he threw her into the pool because she wouldn't stop teasing him about modeling in his shirt, tie, and socks. Then she managed to pull him into the pool. They splashed each other back and forth for a while, until he put his arms around her, as a hold position, in order for her to stop splashing him. In that instant, Sabrina suddenly kissed him.

After that trip he was more confused about his relationship with Jill, and the difference between his feelings for Sabrina and those he had for Jill. He liked Sabrina's spontaneity, and her energetic attitude, as well as the fact that she had the same passion he did for the doll industry. What he didn't know about her whether or not she was a believer in Jesus Christ.

Book club questions for discussion: *Chapters 13-26*

❖ *Do you think Tara had good reasons to be concerned with Brad and Jill's relationship or does she lack confidence in herself? Have you ever felt like Tara in a similar situation? If yes, how did it work out?*

❖ *Sabrina! If you were to describe her outlook on her career, money and relationships what would you say?*

❖ *Where do you think the inner voice or thoughts that Jill talks about comes from?*

❖ *Have you ever quoted scriptures when you're in a stressful or anxious situation like Jill did in Chapter 25? If yes, did it help?*

❖ *What are some of the scriptures that you read or memorize to get you through the rough times?*

Chapter 27

It was a brisk Thanksgiving morning. The hunters—Travis, Bo, and Joe—were out hunting pheasants and rabbits—a tradition for the men in the family. Clara told the girls it was the best way to keep the men out of the kitchen. The best table rabbits were called "jump rabbits." This rabbit would have no buckshot in him, making him easy to fix. Then she told a story about Bo's first hunt with her husband, back when he courted Bobby Sue.

"Grandpa Joe spotted a rabbit sitting in the grass and signaled Bo to jump it. When he went to leap on the rabbit, it jumped out of his hands and kaboom went the gun! There stood Grandpa with a grin from ear to ear. He shot Bo's rabbit. Bo learned later on that it was a set-up. Grandpa knew the rabbit would leap. The grass wasn't tall enough to hide Bo's body when he went to jump on it."

The girls laughed as they gathered in the kitchen to make the side dishes for the dinner. Jill arrived early so she could help. Clara asked her to get the pan of turkey out of the refrigerator and put it in the roaster. This was one of Clara's tricks to make the turkey dinner a little easier. She would roast the turkey a week before the dinner, debone it, arrange it in turkey broth and freeze it. Then she would get it out of the freezer the night before and put it in the refrigerator to thaw. This made it mess-free on Thanksgiving Day.

"We'll heat the turkey in the roaster to free up the oven to cook the side dishes."

Greta made the dough for walnut scones and apricot empanadas while Bobby Sue prepared most of the side dishes. It was pretty easy, as they had frozen most of the seasoned vegetables. Bobby Sue pulled out the long-stemmed green beans and added her favorite, dehydrated cranberries, to the pan, sprinkling garlic salt and a little bit of water to steam them. The corn was next. They had already shucked the frozen ears to cook in a small Crock-Pot with a couple dabs of butter, salt, and pepper. Clara's job was to make her famous sweet potato casserole while

Jill followed the instructions on how to make the green Jell-O dessert as this was Bo's favorite.

Kaboom! Went the shotgun again and again. Each time the girls stopped what they were doing and looked at each other with wide eyes!

Clara was the first to speak. "Now who do you suppose that was?"

Bobby Sue and Greta said in unison. "Grandpa!"

Jill spoke up. "Do you think he got it?"

Clara chuckled. "Well, let's hope so. If not, I'm sure he will have a good story of how it got away."

After Jill made the dessert, she and Greta set the table in the Grand Room.

Jill was the first to speak. "Greta? How close are you to Travis?"

Greta gave a quick laugh. "Well, considering we're two years apart, and were homeschooled from kindergarten through twelfth grade together, I'd say we're like twins. If you think about it, Jill, we've eaten every breakfast, lunch, and supper together with only a few exceptions, until recently. Why do you ask?"

Jill wasn't sure how to continue the conversation as Greta had a straightforward personality. "Well, I know he's been away from home a lot lately with all his travels and I wasn't sure if he's had time to talk to you about what's been going on between us. I mean, we're doing great right now and I only have high hopes that things will get better once I graduate and move back home."

Greta listened as she placed all the drinking glasses on the table, then, without slowing her stride, she said, "You mean about the two of you having different views about children?"

Jill stopped positioning the utensils on each of the napkins, and turned toward Greta with wide eyes and lips pressed tight. "Um—yeah. Wow, he does confide in you."

"Yes, he does. I don't know the reason why you don't want children, but I do know Travis does. I don't think he's opposed to adopting along with his own, The Bible says 'be fruitful and multiply. It's something you could pray about and see how that verse speaks to you and how you can multiply the Kingdom of God."

Jill could scarcely breathe. She had never considered God's view on children. She repeated softly what Greta said, *"Be fruitful and multiply."* *I need to read that section of the Bible and see for myself what God thinks about all this.* She didn't notice that Greta had walked out of the room leaving her to her own thoughts.

***

Thanksgiving dinner was a great success. The men came home with a table rabbit and one pheasant. Tears ran down Jill's cheek as she laughed at the story: Grandpa Joe took the first shot at a pheasant the same moment Travis jumped on a rabbit. The rabbit was big, giving Travis a fight for its life. The two of them wrestled on the ground as Grandpa Joe shot a few more times before the pheasant finally fell. By the time Travis's dad, Bo, looked over at Travis rolling back and forth on the ground, he thought he had been shot by Joe! Once Travis finally got control of the rabbit, he lay still for a few seconds as Bo studied him with concern. Soon Travis stood up with a grin on his face and a prize catch in his hands. With one hand he held the rabbit by its back legs, and gave it a karate chop on the back of its neck with the other hand. This was how he was taught to bring home a table rabbit.

Once everyone was seated they went around the table and shared what they were thankful for. Then, of course, they shared stories of past Thanksgivings with those who hadn't heard them before. Jill loved the way Travis's family made her feel so welcome.

That evening Jill unpacked her luggage remembering what Greta said earlier about the Bible verse, *"be fruitful and multiply."* She looked at her watch, and wondered if it was too late to knock on Travis's grandparents' suite door to borrow a Bible.

Oh, wait, I can Google it on my phone. She grabbed her phone and typed in the words. As she scrolled down, she saw the verse was in Genesis. *Then God blessed Noah and his sons, saying to them, "Be fruitful and increase in number and fill the earth."*

Okay, well, it seems to me that He is talking to Noah and his sons, not to me. Reading through to chapter nine, she read verses seven to nine: *As for you, be fruitful and increase in number; multiply on the earth and increase upon it. Then God said to Noah and to his sons with him: "I now establish my covenant with you and with your descendants after you."*

Jill stopped for a moment then glanced back at verse nine and reread it out loud this time, "I now establish my covenant with you and with your descendants after you. Descendants, descendants, what exactly does that word mean?" She Googled the word and found this phrase: "a person related to someone from an earlier generation."

She continued to talk to herself. *If I'm a believer, wouldn't that make me born from the earlier generation?* Jill felt her stomach clench at the thought. She wasn't sure if she felt confused or convicted about her obligation to bear children, or being submissive to the Word of God. As she clicked off her phone she thought, *I need to pray for wisdom on this.* She quietly prayed and got ready for bed.

Chapter 28

Jill fell asleep thinking about her senior year of high school. It was a Sunday morning in church when her pastor had announced that a mission's team would be going to Russia to help with an orphanage. Once Jill heard the news she knew that she wanted to be a part of the team! Pastor Tom told them that each participant would each need $2,000 to cover the cost of the trip.

Oh, how in the world will I ever come up with that much money? In her own thoughts, doodling on her bulletin, Pastor Tom's voice faded further and further away. With only a part time job at the ice cream shop, she'd have to do some fancy footwork to raise enough money for her parents to agree with her plan.

When she looked back at her bulletin she noticed what she doodled and thought, *Wow, that would look great on a bracelet!* Oh boy, not only did the organ music start up again, her heart started to beat faster as her mind went crazy with thoughts of designs and how to sell her jewelry line to raise the money.

Jill couldn't wait to get home that day to pull out all her jewelry kits. Through the years she had collected a wide variety of beads and crystals.

She peeled off her church clothes and slipped into her favorite zebra crop top and black shorts. She gathered both sides of her hair up on top of her head and clipped it together with a zebra barrette. She had always had an obsession for zebras. *That's it! I'll make zebra slap-on bracelets for the kids at the orphanage!*

Her fundraising campaign came together in her mind as she searched for all the zebra beads and fabrics she had accumulated over the years. *Oh, I'm getting ahead of myself*, she thought. *First I need to design something for my fundraiser. I will design a zebra line of necklaces, matching brooches and earrings, along with a tag explaining that zebras' stripes are unique to each zebra, like fingerprints are to humans. Yes, that's what makes us unique. That's it! My jewelry line will be known as, "Unique One."* She wore a proud grin as she walked toward her vanity. *"I'm just so clever,"* she said to herself in the mirror.

Then she heard her mother's voice. "Jill? Jill, lunch is on the patio. Are you going to join us?"

"Oh yes, I'll be right there!" She switched out her earrings to her zebra dangles, along with her zebra ring.

"Perfect," she said as she ran toward the stairs, grabbing her black scarf.

Seeing her sister, Shannon, walk through the front door with her baby daughter, Ellie Elizabeth, Jill draped her scarf around her neck, then reached for her niece. "Hi, Miss Ellie E., come and see your favorite auntie."

"Not like you're her only aunt," Shannon replied sarcastically.

Jill wrinkled her forehead. "Oh, that's beside the point! Let me see her." She took her in her arms, and Ellie Elizabeth gave her a big smile.

"Oh, wow! Miss Ellie, you're drooling! Uh…well, here! You want her back?"

"Oh Jill, you're ridiculous when it comes to babies," Shannon said. "Yes, she's drooling because she has a tooth coming in. In fact, she's had me up several nights in a row now."

Shannon took Ellie in her arms as she continued, "With Jamar gone on active duty for three more months I don't know if I can handle her on my own."

Shannon and Jill's mom, Marge, grinned as she entered the room. "Aw, little Miss Ellie, you can't help that you're getting a new tooth. Your mama is just going to have to learn to take naps when you do." She leaned over and gave Ellie a kiss, then they made their way toward the patio where Marge's husband, Bob and her mom, Glady Elizabeth, sat.

"Well, hello there, Shannon! My, you look a bit tired today."

Shannon flopped down in a chair beside her dad as she replied, "Oh, Daddy, I'm so tired. Ellie had me up all night!"

Bob chuckled. "I remember those days. Your mom and I would take turns with you girls staying up, rocking you during the night."

"That's just it, Daddy. I'm all by myself!"

Grandma Glady tapped her cane on the floor a few times to get a word in. "Well, back in my day, the husband didn't lift a finger to help out with the babies!"

***

Jill rolled over on her side and realized that the tapping of Grandma Glady's cane was really someone knocking on her door. It was Travis's grandma.

"Jill, are you up?"

Jill shook her head to help wake up from her dream state and sat up, breathing hard. She hurriedly rose to open the door. "Hi, Clara, I'm sorry. How long were you calling my name?"

Clara walked into the room. "Oh, not long. You're fine, honey. We wanted to see if you wanted to have breakfast with us." Jill tried to catch up with reality, and asked if Travis would be joining them as well.

Clara smiled. "He's already downstairs my dear, talking to Grandpa. So, maybe you'd like to meet us there in five minutes?"

Jill smiled and agreed. "Okay, sounds good! Five minutes."

She pulled her hair into a ponytail on top of her head, and wondered why she had relived that part of her past last night.

What is God trying to tell me? I'm so confused! Yes, I was excited to go help the orphan children, and no, I didn't exactly appreciate Ellie Elizabeth's drool. Uh, it only means that I am still confused about my desire for children.

Breakfast included pancakes and a pot of coffee. Although Travis wasn't a coffee drinker, Jill had no problem drinking a cup with his grandparents. They even tried peanut butter on top of their pancakes, the way Jill liked them.

Travis added peanut butter to his pancakes as well, saying, "Nothing beats peanut butter pancakes with warm syrup drizzled over them."

Jill smiled.

Clara asked Jill. "What's next on your adventure list?"

Jill shared the fact that she would be going to New York the same time as Travis, using the ticket she won to the runway show. Meanwhile, Travis and

Grandpa talked about Travis's doll design and how he wanted to present his patent to a reproduction doll company in New York. Grandpa Joe sat quietly nodding his approval. Travis's gaze met Jill's, giving him a yearning desire to be alone with her. He excused them both from the table with hugs of appreciation for the breakfast.

Walking out of the room Travis pulled her in close and kissed the top of her head. "Do you know what I want to do right now?"

Jill giggled as she looked up at him. "Hmm—go to the Zoo's winter wonder lights display?"

With a soft chuckle and a grin Travis said, "No that's not what I had in mind, but maybe later on we could do that. I want to spend some alone time with *just* you!"

She could hardly contain herself. "I'd love that! We have been so busy with your family and Thanksgiving traditions that we haven't had any time to spend alone. So what do you want to do?"

"Being that it's still unseasonably warm outside, how about we grab a quilt and head over to the pond and relax?"

Jill softly moancd, "Mmm—that sounds nice."

Travis smiled. "Maybe later we could canoe around the pond and then go see the Zoo lights."

Jill quickly responded. "Are you serious about going to see the lights tonight?"

"Yep."

Jill squealed as she hugged him, "Travis, you make me so happy. Oh, and about the canoeing, I'll agree to it if only you do all the paddling. I don't want pond water dripping across my lap."

Travis laughed out loud. "Oh Jill, you're one of a kind."

Chapter 29

Jill had hardly gotten in the door before Tara started to share what had happened over Thanksgiving and about the final performance of Oklahoma. What pleased Jill the most was to hear that Brad presented Tara with a dozen red roses on the last curtain call.

"Wow, that was really sweet of Brad!"

Tara smiled. "I know! Then at the casting party that night he went on to tell me that he enjoyed working with me. Oh! Oh! He also said that he would like to take me to a local theater performance during the holidays."

Jill was excited for Tara. "Maybe I should leave more often. It sure seems to bring you good luck."

Tara giggled. "So how was your Thanksgiving with Travis and his family?"

Jill was equally excited about her Thanksgiving holiday. "Well, it was good. I love his family. They made me felt like I belonged. They let me help in the kitchen and shared family stories during dinner." She continued; as her eyes got brighter, her smile grew wider.

"Tara babe, I'm so in love with Travis! We had a wonderful time yesterday. After we had breakfast with his grandparents we spent the rest of the day alone, together."

Tara was curious. "Yeah—do tell. What did you do, alone, together?"

Jill inhaled and slowly let her breath out. "Oh Tara, it wasn't so much what we did; it was the fact that it was just the two of us. We haven't had much alone time since we started dating. With me here in Canton and him in Columbus it makes it hard to get that time we need to get to know each other on a deeper level."

Tara was not satisfied with that answer. "So what did you two do?"

Jill smiled. "We got a quilt and laid it on the ground near their pond and as we lay on the quilt looking at the sky, we talked about…."

Tara blurred out, "Getting married? Did he ask you to marry him?"

Jill lost her train of thought. "What? Where did that come from? No! We talked about things our families did during the holidays when we were growing up."

Tara's tone was decidedly disappointed. "Oh, really? So, that makes you 'so in love with him'?"

Jill nodded. "It was really fun to hear how excited he would get as a kid over the different things they would do. I don't know; it just made me feel closer to him when I understood who he was, growing up. When you're really in love with someone, you want to know everything about them."

Tara smiled. "So I guess I need to let Brad know more about me as a child, so he'll fall head-over-heels in love with me."

Jill shook her head, "I don't think you can make someone fall in love with you. Don't try so hard. Hey, he did ask to take you to a show during the holiday break. That's saying something, right?"

Tara mumbled, "Yeah, I guess so.... Who knows, he probably has an uncle who works at the theater and gets free tickets."

Jill smirked. "Well, if that's true then you would probably be able to get free popcorn!"

Tara quickly snapped a look at Jill and they both laughed.

Chapter 30

That night the weather took an extreme change for the worse. Indian summer was long gone and the threat of snow was in the forecast. Jill was packed and ready to fly out to New York for the Winter Runway Show. Travis had been in New York for most of the week and the plans were for the two of them to meet on his last day and see a little of New York before flying home together. Even though she would only have a half day with Travis, Jill was excited when she boarded the plane to New York.

***

The waitress at the café beside the New York airport asked Jill if she would like more tea.

"Oh, yes, please. I'm sorry. I was lost in my own thoughts." Earlier Jill saw on the TV monitor that the city had declared a level three travel ban due to the snowstorm. After the waitress poured the tea, Jill thanked her. "Do you know how long the city will be shut down?"

The waitress looked over Jill's head at the monitor. "It says that the winter weather advisory will not be lifted until tomorrow at two p.m."

Jill sighed. "Thank you." She was concerned that Travis might not be able to meet her as planned. They were to celebrate his new production line before they headed back home from New York.

"Oh, one more thing. Could you recommend a place for me to stay tonight?" The waitress started to recommend a place when Jill's attention drifted toward a lady who walked into the diner with three small children. They were huddled deep into their coats with snow caked on their scarves and mittens. She turned her attention back to the waitress and thanked her for the information. The waitress smiled and nodded.

The rosy-cheeked children whined that they were cold. Their mother tried to comfort them, saying that as soon as they took seats in a nearby booth, she would order them some warm soup. Jill could feel the wintry draft waft over her as they walked by. The youngest child, who looked about five, struggled with the buttons on her coat.

When she looked at Jill with a pleading look, it reminded her of Alex, a little boy at the orphanage in Lomonosov, Russia.

He was assigned to Jill as someone who would need extra attention during art class. Jill had successfully raised her missionary funding by designing and selling her own jewelry line. She was the perfect choice to create an art project for the orphan children. Jill wanted them to know the Father in heaven had designed and made each of them special, with a one-of-a-kind destiny. Along with the souvenir zebra snap bracelets for the children, she had bags full of five different color beads and leather strings to make necklaces while she shared the story of Jesus. Each of the five colored beads represented a different part of Jesus' story. The children put the necklaces together and then wore them as remembrance chokers.

Jill felt a tug on her sweater from the youngest of the three girls. She asked Jill if she could unbutton her coat, because her fingers weren't working.

"Oh, why certainly! I can help you with that! Your fingers must be so cold that you can't even feel them."

The little girl sighed. "Uh huh."

"Well here, wrap your little fingers around my cup of hot tea, to help warm you up." The other two girls also needed help, so she invited them to sit in her booth, stretching out her dry coat over their laps. The waitress came over to her table with the children's soup. Jill asked where their mother had gone. The waitress said that she was on the office phone trying to make arrangements for a place to stay the night.

"Oh, that's right! I have to find a place to stay too." Just then the mother walked out of the office.

"I'm so sorry," she said as she hurried toward Jill's table. "I—I... told the kids to sit down. I thought they would grab their own booth."

"Oh, that's okay. I invited for them to sit with me while they waited on their food."

She looked at her kids then back at Jill. "Are you sure?"

With a warm smile, Jill replied, "Yes, I'm sure." She could see the woman's shoulders relax a little when she let out a deep breath, but Jill could still see sadness in her eyes.

"Here." Jill patted the bench seat. "Have some tea. I have plenty in the teapot." She moved over as the waitress offered to bring a second tea cup.

While the kids slurped their soup, Jill introduced herself and learned that the mother's name was Sarah. "Have you found a place to stay for the night?" she asked.

"No," Sarah replied, "everything is booked due to the airport shut down."

Jill looked over at the kids. "Oh no, we should have prayed over the soup with thanksgiving and asked for guidance about where we should stay for the night."

Sarah flashed Jill a look of disbelief, and with that, Jill turned her attention back to the children. "Hey girls, let's put our hands together and bow our heads with our eyes closed. I want to pray for all of us. *'Dear Jesus, thank You for this wonderful family that You brought to my table, when I was feeling quite alone and wondering where to stay in this storm. It's a great comfort Lord, knowing You brought us together and that You will see us through this. Thank You that this diner was open and for the warm food we're enjoying. Now we need direction regarding where to stay tonight. In Jesus' name, amen.'*

Jill looked up to see the kids staring at her. She kindly said, "Now it's your turn to say amen."

In unison they said, "Amen!"

Sarah didn't say a word, but the look on her face had softened when the waitress approached their table, saying, "My boss called and told me to close up early due to the storm. He also invited me to stay in the warm upstairs apartment.

Knowing your situation, I would like to invite you upstairs to stay with me. By the way, my name is Wanda."

Jill glanced up at the ceiling. "Thank You, Lord, and thank you, Wanda! Yes, that would be wonderful! I—I—mean…" She turned to look at Sarah. "What do you think?"

The kids suddenly bounced up and down in their seat, and one said, "Yes, Mommy! We like her, she's really nice."

Jill smiled then stuck her hand out to officially greet Sarah. "I'd love to have a slumber party with you and your family!"

Sarah shook her hand wearing a tired smile. "Yes, thank you. We would be very grateful to stay here with you." The kids squealed as they hugged each other.

Chapter 31

Before Jill opened her eyes the next morning, she said a silent prayer of thanks. She thought she was the first one to wake up, until the smell of coffee caught her attention. She looked around and noticed that the waitress was gone, but she had left coffee, milk, and pastries on the table. Jill smiled and rolled on her side thinking how the girls were so excited about the sleepover. In her mind she replayed the adventure of getting the girls' PJs on and tucking them in bed with pillows and blankets. Meanwhile, she wondered if she could enjoy kids of her own. Travis hadn't mentioned children since they got back together after Homecoming. He'd been busy with his doll line so she could only hope he wouldn't dwell on it, or he might decide to end their relationship for good, as past boyfriends had.

Oh! Jill thought. *What time is it?* She flung off her blankets and carefully picked her way over the sleeping children and found her phone. It was nine thirty.

Still puzzled about the meaning of being fruitful, she searched the web on her phone and typed in fruitfulness and read John 15:16, 17. *You did not choose Me, but I chose you and appointed you so that you might go and bear fruit—fruit that will last—and so that whatever you ask in My name the Father will give you. This is My command: Love each other.*

The kids started to stir and grumbled that they were hungry. Jill hurriedly turned off her phone and whispered quietly, "Shh, your mom is still asleep. But the waitress left us some pastries and milk. Come to the table and help yourself."

Jill looked over to where Sarah was asleep and wondered what her story was. She had clearly seen the sadness and fatigue in her eyes the previous night, but Sarah looked peaceful now.

Jill said another quick prayer. *Dear Lord, please use me as a tool to let Sarah see You, and to feel Your love and presence here. In Jesus' name, amen.*

The oldest child, whose name was Tessa, looked out the window at the snow-covered town. "Wow, I have never seen so much snow in my whole life, and I'm nine years old!" The other two girls, Elise and Aubrey, ran to the window with pastries in hand.

As she smacked her chest with her free hand, Elise said, "I have never seen so much snow in my life either, and I'm only seven!"

"Me either, and I'm only five!" Aubrey added. They all giggled.

Jill couldn't help herself. She picked up her phone and started taking pictures of the girls as they looked out the window in awe of the beauty of fresh white snow.

Aubrey heard the camera click and said, "Hey, take a picture of this." She stuck her tongue out near the window and acted like she was catching snowflakes with her tongue.

Elise said, "No, take a picture of me." She opened up the window and grabbed a handful of snow off the windowsill, packed it into a snowball, and threw it at Tessa!

"Ooh, that does it!" Tessa exclaimed. She threw down her pastry to grab some snow and started to throw it back at Elise. Jill giggled when Aubrey joined in on the snowball fight.

Suddenly they heard Sarah. "Oh, no! What are you girls doing?" The three girls stopped and looked at Sarah.

"Mommy, you're awake!" They replied, jumping on Sarah's bed. Jill used the opportunity to take more photos of the fun.

Chapter 32

Without phone reception, Travis was concerned about how to make contact with Jill. The last time he talked to her was the day she boarded the plane for New York. Once she landed, she texted him and said the flight was terrible due to the heavy snowfall, and that she was going to treat herself to some hot tea at a diner near the airport.

Looking out the window from his suite, on the top floor of the new five-star hotel that the production company had booked for the week, Travis could see city workers plow some of the major roadways. *Well, that's encouraging,* he thought. *The worst of the storm must be over and now it's time to get the city up and running again.*

He planned to see some of New York with Jill before flying home together so he needed to get in touch with her. He went down to the front desk and explained his situation and asked the clerk if there were a lot of diners near the airport. "No, as a matter of fact there is only one and the rest are fast-food restaurants."

"Awesome! Now, how can I get to this diner?"

"Well sir," the man behind the desk continued, "we're going to have to do some creative thinking. We're under a level three travel emergency in the city until they can open the main roads."

"Ugh." Travis sighed. "Does the hotel have its own snow removal equipment?"

"Well, yes sir, we do," he responded. "However, the guy who operates it is snowed in at home."

Travis stood there for a minute considering other options. Then, with a snap of his fingers, he said, "That's it! What if I plow your parking lot in exchange for borrowing your truck to pick up my girl?"

The clerk, a little stunned, said, "Oh! Well—uh—I don't know. Do you know how to handle a plow truck?"

Travis eagerly replied, "Yes, sir. I've been plowing snow since I was sixteen years old!"

The clerk swayed back and forth, rubbing his chin. "Umm, sir, I don't think I should. There is too much liability at stake here."

Travis tried not to show his disappointment. "I understand." He sighed as he turned away and carried on to the restaurant where he took a seat at a table by the window.

"Good morning, sir. Will you be eating from the breakfast bar?" The waitress asked as she poured a glass of water.

Travis looked from the window to the waitress, and smiled. "Yes please, and oh, can I get a copy of the *Wall Street Journal*?"

"Yes, sir. You may help yourself to the breakfast bar as soon as you're ready, and I'll be right back with the paper."

Travis nodded then reached into his pocket to check the phone service. Disappointed, he tucked his phone back into his pocket and headed to the breakfast bar.

As he waited his turn, he overheard a couple in front of him talk about their last trip to New York City, and how they loved the horse and carriage ride they took. *Hmm,* Travis thought, *that sounds pretty cool. Jill would love to do something like that.*

Filling his plate, he was all about the pancakes and the different flavors of syrup. When the waitress brought the *Journal*, he asked her if she would bring him some peanut butter.

She looked at his plate full of pancakes and frowned. "Peanut butter, sir?"

Travis chuckled. "Yeah, my girlfriend got me started on peanut butter and maple syrup on my pancakes."

"Well, that's a new one on me. I'll be right back with your peanut butter."

Travis opened the newspaper and noticed there wasn't much going on since the last time he looked at it. He set the paper aside as the waitress came back with the peanut butter.

Finished with breakfast, Travis looked around and saw the couple that was in front of him at the breakfast bar. He got up and walked toward them eager to learn more about the carriage ride.

"Excuse me, but I overheard you mention a carriage ride. I wanted to ask you a little more about it. By the way, my name is Travis Gunner."

"Oh, yes, we enjoyed it tremendously." The woman said. She motioned for Travis to sit down then introduced themselves as Hannah and Jeremy Walsh.

An idea came to him once he heard about their ride. "How far is the carriage stand?"

Hannah swallowed a sip of her coffee. "Oh, not far at all. It's on the street behind the hotel. Actually, you can see it from the pool room."

"You don't suppose the stable manager would be there now, do you?"

Jeremy and Hannah looked at each other, then at Travis. Jeremy spoke up first. "I would think so. An elderly couple, Annabelle and Edwin own it, and live in a section just off the stables."

When Travis explained his situation, Hannah suggested he should go to the pool room and look for lights on or activity at the stables.

Travis started to feel hopeful. "Actually, that's a great idea. It's not too far. Maybe I can borrow a shovel and scoop a path to their place. Thanks for the help. It was nice to talk with you. I hope you have a safe trip home."

"Thank you. You too!" Hannah Added. "I hope you get to your loved one."

Travis paid for his breakfast then headed back to the front desk. He was on a mission. He had to get to Jill and make sure she was all right.

Chapter 33

Jill wanted to take the girls outside and make snow friends. She asked Sarah if it would be okay, and Sarah replied, "Oh, I don't want them to bother you."

"Oh, no, I think it will be fun!" Jill said. "I love to play in the snow. When I was younger, my younger sister and I would make snow friends. We had so much fun. We dressed our snow friends up, too. I brought extra clothes and thought Wanda may have some food coloring and a spray bottle to make hair coloring and make-up."

Jill was excited as she went to find the waitress. She found her in the main floor kitchen looking over her menu for the week. When she noticed Jill, she stood up and said, "Oh, I'm sorry. Do you need something?"

"No, I want to say thank you for the nice breakfast you left upstairs for us," Jill replied, "…and, well, hmm...."

Wanda gave her a half smile. "And...?"

Jill laughed. "Well, since you have no customers and the kids are getting restless upstairs, I thought we could go outdoors and build snow friends. You know, like snowmen?"

Wanda said, "Okay, but what do you need from me?"

"You see…." Jill went on to explain the need for food coloring, to make their snow friends colorful. Wanda liked the idea and gathered the supplies she would need.

Chapter 34

Travis was wearing the hotel custodian's muck boots when he walked over to the stable. He was full of hope that someone would be home as he approached the barnyard. He smelled the familiar smell of manure and knew he was in the right place. A Clydesdale stuck his head out the window, and Travis reached up and rubbed his head.

"Hey there, buddy!" The horse nickered softly and lowered his head, enjoying the affection. Fresh hay in the horse's stall meant someone had recently been there. Travis went to the barn door and opened it with a greeting, "Hello, anyone here?"

The horses lifted their heads to see who was talking.

A woman he assumed was Annabelle left the tack room with her hands full of harness equipment with her husband, Edwin, following close behind.

"Oh, Edwin, this will be fun, taking the boys out in this new snow, once all the main streets are plowed. I think the wind has died down too! I'll get Billy and you get Bob so that—Oh!" Annabelle squealed as she saw Travis standing in the aisle. She was so startled that she dropped Billy's harness.

Travis immediately knelt down to pick up the gear with an apologetic tone. "I'm sorry to have startled you!"

When Edwin saw Travis, he put down the load he carried and motioned for Annabelle to step behind him. He reassured her that he would take care of the intruder. He then turned to Travis. "Excuse me, but what are you doing in here?"

Travis slowly stood and reached out his hand. "My name is Travis Gunner, sir," and in an apologetic tone, he added. "I am in need of transportation to find my girlfriend!"

Annabelle peeked around Edwin with an open mouth. "Whaaat!? What do you mean? Where did you last see her?"

Travis went on, "I heard about your carriage business and walked over from the hotel to see if there would be any way I could somehow use your service to find my girlfriend, Jill."

"Oh, Edwin!" Annabelle said as he turned and put his arm around her.

"Now, honey, calm down. Let's hear the boy out." Edwin looked back at Travis. "Go on, son. Finish with what you came for."

Travis explained that he hadn't been able to contact Jill by phone. He hadn't even finished the story when they started to get the horses ready to go.

Annabelle noticed that Travis was comfortable around horses and asked if he had experience with horses. Travis told her about his family's horse farm back in Ohio.

"I got my first horse when I was four. I showed horses for a while and now I enjoy riding them around the ranch."

Annabelle smiled and interjected that she, too, had been raised with horses.

Edwin demonstrated how to hook up the carriage then said. "Let's go find your gal!"

The three of them climbed into the carriage with a blanket over their laps and off they went with Billy and Bob snorting and prancing, eager to go.

As they approached the side streets leading to the diner, they saw that the roads had yet to be cleared. The snow was unusually deep, halfway to the top of the carriage wheels, making it slow going for the horses who lowered their heads and used their shoulders to plow.

Annabelle asked Edwin, "Whatcha thinkin?"

As he pulled the team to a halt, he replied, "Hmm. Well, I'm afraid it's going to put a lot of stress on the carriage axle. We have two choices. One is to wait for the plows to clear the side roads, or two, unhitch the horses and ride them to find Jill."

"Oh, Edwin!" exclaimed Annabelle. "Neither of those options will work. We can't wait! And we're far too old to ride on a big Clydesdale, for Pete's sake!"

Just then Travis spoke up. "Okay look, I know you don't know me but I'm really grateful for your help. What if we make a simple sled for them to pull that doesn't need wheels?"

Edwin was silent for a few seconds and then his face lit up in a smile. "By George, I think I've got it!" He commanded Billy and Bob to turn around, so they could head back to the barn.

Book club questions for discussion.   *Chapters 27-34*

❖ *In Chapter 27, Greta mentioned, "be fruitful and multiply" to Jill and advised her to read about it, to see what it meant to her. What are your thoughts on Genesis chapter 1-9?*

❖ *Jill fell asleep after reading and pondering Genesis chapters 1-9 and dreamed of her past while working with orphaned children and dealing with her niece's drool. Do you think it was the Holy Spirit or her subconscious mind revealing the indecisiveness about having children?*

❖ *Do you think the Holy Spirit can and will speak to you through your dreams? If yes, how do you know it is from Him?*

Chapter 35

Tessa put the final touch on their snow friends with orange, purple, and lime green food coloring. Meanwhile, the two younger girls watched Jill, and following her example, lying down in the snow and waving their arms and legs to make angel wings. Then they repeated the design in a circle around the snow friends.

Jill wanted a picture of what she and the girls had created so she ran into the diner to see if Sarah would come out and take a picture of them with her phone. Sarah bundled up and followed Jill out the front door. "It touches me to see my girls so happy and proud of their snow art. In fact, I haven't felt such joy in a long time. It actually gives me hope to see the angels surrounding the little snow people with their wild-colored hair."

Tessa ran up to Sarah wearing a wide smile. "Look, Mommy, this is our family, and now that we met Jill, we know that there are angels all around us."

Though Sarah looked confused she said, "Is that so?" She turned to watch Jill position the girls inside the circle of snow angels.

The waitress ran out of the diner. "I've been watching through the window and thought I should take the picture so Sarah could be in the picture too."

The girls yelled, "Yeah, Mommy, get in the picture with us!" Sarah stood with Jill and the girls. Wanda was just about ready to snap the picture when they heard the sound of nearby thunder. The sound grew louder with the addition of neighing horses. Click went the camera, with all eyes on Billy and Bob.

Jill could scarcely believe her eyes: Travis stood behind the big draft horses, pulling a very unusual contraption—himself on a snow sled!

"O Travis, I'm so happy to see you!" She ran toward him and jumped into his arms, hugging him like there was no tomorrow.

As Travis tried to balance on the sled, Jill giggled as she jumped down and noticed what he had on—muck boots with his suit pants tucked into them, along with his black picot jacket, while standing on the sled with a set of harness leathers in his hand. Beside him was an older gentleman also standing on his own sled.

"Travis! What are you doing here like this?"

"Well, as you can imagine, Jill, I was concerned about you when I couldn't get through to you by phone. Edwin here…" Travis smiled at the older man, "was kind enough to hitch up Billy and Bob to find you."

Jill giggled as she looked down at the sleds attached to the horses' harness. "On two small snow sleds? Wow!"

Edwin chuckled and chimed in, "Well—it's a complicated story but let's just say we're glad to see you!" The waitress, Sarah, and all the kids gathered around them, laughing and petting Billy and Bob.

Wanda still had Jill's phone, so she stepped back and took a few pictures of the whole gang, then announced, "This one is going on the diner wall, along with the picture of the snow friends encircled by the snow angels."

She looked over at Sarah who had rested her head against Billy's jaw while she gently held his big head in her arms. Billy seemed to enjoy it as he lowered his head and closed his eyes. Sarah inhaled a deep breath of horse scent while slowly petting his face. Her eyes were also closed when she smiled, as if she were somewhere else entirely.

Chapter 36

Jill beamed as she sat next to Travis on the flight home from New York. She held his hand, resting her head on his shoulder.

She looked up with a loving smile and he met her gaze. Wide-eyed, he asked. "What?"

"Oh, nothing. Well, okay—everything." She sighed aloud then went on, "I'm disappointed that I didn't get to see the fashion show, but it was worth the winter storm to see you in that getup behind the horses."

Travis grinned. "Yeah, well I was concerned for you, out on your own in New York."

"See, I knew you were my knight in shining armor. You came and rescued me."

"I was glad to see that you were all right and not alone. By the way, what's Sarah's story? Where was she traveling to with three young children?"

"She said she was going to stay with an elderly aunt until she could figure things out. I'm not sure what that meant because the girls interrupted us and we never talked about it again. We did exchange numbers though and I told her I would stay in touch."

Travis could tell by the look on her face that she was lost in her own thoughts. "Is there more?"

Jill blinked and added, "I don't think she prays."

Travis's eyes grew wide with interest. "What makes you think that?"

Jill lowered her voice, "Well, I remember praying for our food and expressing how grateful I was to have them with me while we waited out the storm. I asked for wisdom about where we should stay that night. When I finished praying, with, 'In Jesus name, amen,' she looked at me with a blank expression, like…she couldn't believe her ears. That's when Wanda, the waitress came to our table and offered to let all of us to stay in the upstairs apartment with her."

Travis sat up straighter in his seat. "Oh that's how you got to know them. Wow, I didn't realize you all were stuck at the diner together for that length of time. But hey, I think that's pretty cool that your prayer was answered."

Jill smiled. "I think so, too!" That night, as we were making up the beds, she asked if I really believed that my prayer had enabled us to get the apartment above the diner, or if it was pure luck. That's why I'm wondering whether she believes."

Travis squeezed her knee as the plane jolted. The pilot came over the speaker explaining that they hit a cold mass of air but that everything was now under control. Jill rested her head on Travis' shoulder and sat quietly looking through the Bible on her phone. As she read John chapter 15 again, her spirit was jolted just as she herself had been jolted on the plane when flying through the cold mass. She finally understood what fruitfulness is. The New Testament of the Bible spoke to her, saying that we are to glorify God, as we spiritually grow and lead others to come to know Him. Content in her own thoughts, she felt that God meant all along for her to meet Sarah and her daughters. A peaceful feeling came over her. She was multiplying God's fruit by being "fruitful," sharing her love of God with them, in hopes that they would grow to love Him too. The Bible verse that Greta had asked her to pray about came to mind. Be fruitful and multiply. *So this is how I can multiply the Kingdom—Spiritually.* Suddenly, she felt a lift in her spirit as the flight attendant announced that they would be descending for the landing and asked that everyone put their seats in the upright position and buckle their seat belts.

Chapter 37

Jill listened to the thunderstorm roll in while sitting on the covered porch of her sorority house. It set the perfect mood as she pondered the many things going on in her life. It was her last week at the house before she graduated, after which she would prepare to enter the job market.

She looked over her list of guests, eager to see everyone at her graduation party in two weeks. Then a wave of sadness enveloped her remembering that she hadn't told Travis that her current employer had offered her a full-time permanent position. Accepting the job would mean traveling and living permanently in Canton, two and a half hours away from him. On a separate sheet of paper, she began soul searching and putting it in a letter to Travis. A letter she wasn't sure she would ever give him. Looking back at her list she noticed Sarah's name.

Hmmm, I wonder how she and the girls are doing. Maybe I'll give her a call. She picked up her phone and placed a call.

"Hello?"

"Sarah? It's me, Jill. How are you and the girls doing?"

Sarah's tone was filled with surprise. "Jill, is it really you? Wow, I thought I would never hear from you after you were rescued by your knight in shining armor!"

Jill laughed as she thought back to where they met—in a diner by the New York airport, where they were trapped in a snowstorm, before she was rescued by a team of Clydesdales pulling Travis on snow sleds.

"How are you guys doing?" The phone was quiet for a long moment.

Sarah responded in a barely audible voice. "Jill, things aren't so good here. The aunt that I planned to stay with is being moved to a nursing home and the bank is foreclosing on her home."

Jill's mind instantly went into rescue mode. "Oh Sarah, I'm so sorry! What are your plans? Where are you and the girls going to go?"

Sarah sighed aloud. "I don't know. The girls remind me every day that there are angels watching over us, like the ones they made in the snow at the diner. But there aren't many options for us right now. I'm afraid I'm losing hope."

Jill still didn't know Sarah's story but felt that it wasn't the right time to ask.

"You know, the girls are right. Let me do some praying and see what I can come up with. Are you opposed to leaving New York?"

Sarah quickly replied, "No, home is where my children are."

She smiled at her description of home. Once Jill reassured Sarah that through prayer she would seek direction from God, she ended the call.

Prayerfully, Jill thought of the Gunner's bed and breakfast. She couldn't wait to talk to Travis about it. But first things first. She needed to talk to him about the job offer she'd received. Jill planned to tell him everything when he came up on the weekend, to help her move back home after the graduation ceremony.

Chapter 38

Travis was closely inspecting the first doll he'd manufactured for the trade show when Jill called. "Hi Jill, I was just thinking about you."

"Yeah, what were you thinking about?"

Travis chuckled. "Well, I can't tell you. But I have a surprise for you. You'll have to wait until I see you this weekend."

Jill was hopeful that he would give her a ring for graduation. "Did you buy it from a place that sells shiny things?"

Travis hesitantly replied, "No, not exactly. But I will say it will be unique like your jewelry design, Unique One. It's definitely one of a kind."

Jill's mind raced, trying to imagine what it was. "Travis, you know I don't do well with waiting!"

He laughed. "Didn't they teach you patience in college? You'll see it soon enough. Your big celebration will be here before you know it."

As romantic thoughts ran through her head, Jill asked, "Are you going to give it to me in private?"

Travis pondered the question before answering. "You'll just have to wait and see."

Jill groaned. "Okay. Hey, speaking of the party, my mom wants to know how soon she and Brad's mom can come by and decorate the Grand Room."

Travis, a little confused, questioned her. "Brad's mom?"

With a sigh Jill replied, "Yes—remember? My mom and Brad's mom are best friends and they wanted to give us a single party because we're graduating from the same college, and most of our friends will attend both parties. So why not party together?"

"Oh, that's right. You did say something about that. Yeah, sure, I'll check with my mom and have her call your mom."

"Oh, great! Well, I can't wait to see you this weekend. I have something important to discuss with you."

Now Travis was curious. "Hmm...well, I look forward to hearing what you have to tell me. I'll see you soon."

***

Bobby Sue and her mother, Clara, were on the porch at the bed and breakfast working on new inspirational decorations for the wall. Smiling, Bobby Sue lifted the old wood-framed window from her painting table.

"It's finished!" She turned it toward her mother so she could see the painted script on the glass pane.

"This is the scripture verse I prayed over my children during their teenage years."

Clara looked up from her quilt and read the scripture aloud: *"May God himself, the God of peace, sanctify you through and through. May your whole spirit, soul and body be kept blameless at the coming of our Lord Jesus Christ. The one who calls you is faithful, and He will do it. 1 Thessalonians 5:23-24."*

"Well, that's very nice. Your prayer must have worked, since both of my grandchildren turned out great, with fine Christian character."

"Thanks, Mom." Just then they heard a car drive up the lane. Bobby Sue squinted to block the glare from the sunlight as she walked down the steps to the parking area.

"Marge and Carol are here!"

Clara set aside her quilt to greet the ladies with a hug, then carried boxes of decorations into the bed and breakfast to decorate the Grand Room for the graduation party.

Chapter 39

Tara and Brad walked into the Palace Theater in Canton, amazed by the grandeur of the building and excited by the offer they got after the final performance of Oklahoma. Mr. Hook introduced them to the producer from the downtown theater. He had complimented their performance and offered them a tryout for the summer production of "Seven Brides for Seven Brothers."

Tara's neck was blotchy red from all the excitement and her own anxious feelings. She whispered to Brad, "Do you think we'll get parts?"

Brad grinned. "I don't know, maybe. Would you like to be partnered with me again?"

Tara's heart began to pound so loudly that she could hear it in her own ears. Eagerly she replied, "Yes, I would because I don't know a single person here. I feel comfortable with you."

Brad lean toward her, smiling, "Is that your only reason?"

Tara wasn't sure how to answer. Suddenly she felt him nudge her with his elbow. She jumped. "What?"

Brad laughed. "I'm kidding. I was trying to lighten the mood. Let's head on in."

Tara drew in a deep breath and slowly exhaled.

The actors in the auditorium were chatting amiably. Tara, full of nervous energy, grabbed Brad's arm, stopping him in his tracks. He could see the fear in her eyes.

"Hey, Listen Tara, it will be okay. You were wonderful in Oklahoma and you're going to be wonderful here." He pulled her close and gave her a hug, and she wrapped her arms around his waist. As she breathed in the smell of his cologne, she could feel herself relax.

Brad began to gently rock back and forth, then kissed the top of her forehead, and gently pushed away from her, still holding her hands. "You okay now?"

Tara nodded. "Thank you, Brad, for the compliment and your confidence in me. I won't let you down."

Chapter 40

Clara made a pitcher of fresh lemonade while Marge and Carol decorated the Grand Room for the graduates. Marge giggled as she hung pink and blue streamers from the ceiling.

"Jill is going to love this theme! Barbie and Ken."

Carol replied, "Now, Marge, that's got to remain our little secret. As far as the kids are concerned, the color scheme just includes their favorite colors."

Marge nodded. "I know. I can remember when they were small we used to say that maybe someday they'd grow up and get married."

Carol stopped adding glass rocks to the vases for the candles as she glanced at the open doorway, before turning her gaze back to Marge, who stood on a ladder. "I think Brad is still holding out for Jill."

Marge held onto the top of the ladder and quietly gasped. "You don't really think so, do you?"

Carol slowly nodded. "I do. Many nice girls have shown interest in him but he's never really pursued any of them."

Marge sighed aloud. "Jill said that Tara—that's her roommate—has a crush on him. You know, she's the girl who played the part of Annie in the musical Oklahoma."

"He hasn't said anything that would indicate he's interested in her. When he comes home from college on weekends, he usually talks about Jill."

They were lost in their own thoughts as Clara walked into the room with glasses of lemonade. "Would you girls like some nice cold drinks?"

Thankful that she hadn't overheard their conversation—they agreed it was a great time for a break.

Marge looked at the clock and reminded Carol that they needed to meet Travis in half an hour to drive up to Canton. Carol agreed and thanked Clara for allowing them to come and decorate a week early.

Clara smiled. "Oh, no problem. We haven't officially opened up to the public yet, because we have to do some renovations. The Grand Room will be waiting for the arrival of your guests next week.

Chapter 41

Jill, Jackie, and Sadie couldn't wait for Tara to return from her Palace Theater audition. But Sadie was actually more concerned than excited.

Jackie sensed her anxiety. "Oh Sadie, don't worry about her. As good as she was in Oklahoma, I'm sure she'll be just as successful in this production."

Sadie blew out a long breath. "Yeah, I know, but tonight is our graduation ceremony, and no matter what happened at the Palace, I hope she'll be able to enjoy herself tonight. I mean this is it, girls. We're graduating from college!"

They started hootin' and hollerin' as they sat on the couch in the living room, when suddenly they heard a whistle. They stopped and looked behind them and saw Tara in the doorway waving a piece of paper in her hand. With a big grin, she said, "Well, is anyone going to ask me how my audition went?"

Jill responded first. "You got the lead part of Milly?"

Tara laughed as she plopped down in the recliner. "I wish! I got the part of Dorcas and Brad got the part as Benjamin. This means, ladies...that we'll be coupled again in this production. Yeek!" She pulled back the recliner handle on her chair and scissor-kicked her feet in the air. "I'm so excited I can hardly wait." The girls all hugged and congratulated her.

Jackie suddenly ran toward the kitchen, returning with four glasses of sparkling grape juice.

She handed each of them a glass as she explained, "I was going to save this for tonight to make a toast and a farewell speech after our graduation ceremony but..." she looked over at Tara, "this is the time to celebrate! Congratulations, Tara!"

The girls held up their glasses, and Jill added, "I know you'll be awesome in this play too!" They clinked glasses. "Hip-hip hooray!"

Tara slipped out of the recliner and took a bow. "Thank you, ladies. I have nothing but great appreciation for my number one fans." She giggled then added, "In fact, since you're my closest friends and only fans, I can't help but share my excitement. Today in my most anxious moment, Brad pulled me into his arms and kissed my forehead!"

Jackie held her glass in the air. "Another toast! Hip hip hooray!"

Sadie stood and added, "Well, ladies, I hate to break up this celebration, but, it's time to get ready for the ceremony. Just think, after we leave here tonight we will come back as accomplished graduates."

***

That evening after the graduation ceremony Travis led Jill outside to the water fountain on campus where he wanted to give her his graduation gift.

As he blindfolded her, she giggled. "Travis, how far do I have to walk blindfolded?"

"We're almost there."

Once they stopped, he asked her to stand still until he was ready.

Jill giggled. "Okay, but hurry. I can hardly wait another minute!"

Travis took a small quilt out of his bag, arranged it on the grass, then removed two bottles of sparkling water and set them on the grass just at the edge of the brick walkway that encircled the fountain. He then placed the doll, a perfect replica of Jill, in a stand, up on the wall of the fountain. It was a magical place to display his first doll, with the lights in the water changing colors in the evening light. He stood beside Jill and guided her to the quilt, and then asked her to kneel and keep her eyes closed while he removed the blindfold. The doll was the first thing she would see when she opened her eyes.

"Ready?"

Jill was about to explode with wonder. "Yes, Travis I'm ready!"

He stood behind her and removed the blindfold. Jill blinked a few times to focus her eyes, then gasped. "Oh, Travis, is that a mini-me?"

Travis chuckled. "Yes, it sure is! It's the first doll of my collection!"

Jill ran over and grabbed the doll off the fountain wall. She ran her hands gently over the face and hair and smiled. "I love it!"

She turned to him and gave him a big kiss and a hug. Travis sent a text to her mother to let her and the rest of the family know that they could come over and see the surprise. Moments later everyone gathered to admire the mini-me doll. Once everybody had taken pictures of the doll the happy couple knelt on the quilt to toast the release of the doll and Jill's graduation with sparkling water.

Chapter 42

The next morning was an emotional one for the girls. Jackie helped Jill pack up the last few boxes, while Sadie and Tara hauled them out to Jill's car to be loaded. Sadie planned to move out at the end of the following weekend, while Tara would continue to rent the house until the end of summer, to accommodate the daily dance classes and play rehearsals for "Seven Brides for Seven Brothers." Jackie's family lived in the area, so she offered to stay in the house with Tara until after the musical ended.

Travis pulled up to the house in his dad's truck with Brad in the passenger seat. He'd stayed at Brad's place after the graduation ceremony, and now they were there to load up Jill's furniture and large pieces to move home.

Jill ran over to Travis after he parked the truck at the curb. "Hi Travis, Brad!"

Travis stepped out of the truck with a yawn and gave Jill a hug. "Well, you're perky today. Are you ready to load up and mosey on down the highway?"

"Yes, I am! I'm going to ride with you while my mom and Carol drive my car home."

The guys loaded up her bed, dresser, as well as containers loaded with shoes, purses, coats, and miscellaneous things while Jackie, Sadie, Tara, and Brad hugged each other goodbye.

With misty eyes, Jill said, "Okay, this is not really goodbye, since I'll see you all next weekend at our party. Right, Brad?" She shuffled over to Brad and gave him a second hug.

He hugged her back. "Yes, that's right. You can't get rid of me that easily."

Everyone laughed except Tara, who just smiled.

Jill gave each of the girls one last hug, then she jumped into the truck and yelled out the window as they pulled away, "So long! I'll see you in one week!"

***

Jill was excited about her future. Her feet were ready to hit the ground running. She was full of confidence after working all year for the company that had just offered her full-time employment. She cleared her throat unsure how to bring up this subject with Travis.

Momentarily she said, "Travis?"

He glanced over at her. "Yeah?"

Jill squirmed in her seat. "Do you remember how I told you that my boss really liked me?"

Travis's eyebrows lifted in surprise. "Yeah, go on."

Jill quickly replied, "Well, I'm just going to say it! They offered me a full-time position with an increase in pay and benefits!"

Travis's eyes grew wide as he met her gaze. "What? Really? You're kidding me!"

Jill couldn't stifle a nervous chuckle. "No, I'm serious. But they said I could have a few months to think about it since I just graduated. They want me to make sure that if I accept the position, it won't be on impulse."

Travis nodded in agreement. "Hmm, well, I agree that you shouldn't make a rash decision. What are you thinking?"

"Well, I'd love it! I already know everyone there and I love the position they offered me. Of course, I'd be traveling a lot. You know how I love to travel, and why not, if they're paying for it."

Travis was quiet, taking it all in. Momentarily he asked, "So they gave you the summer to think about it?"

Jill nodded. "It's like offering me a vacation without pay before giving me a new position with a pay increase."

"It sounds like a great opportunity!"

Lost in their own thoughts, neither of them said a word for the next half hour. Finally, Jill broke the silence. "Travis, can we stop and get a smoothie or something light to eat?"

He looked in his rearview mirror to see if her mother was still behind them. "Sure. Do you want to call your mom to see if they want to stop too?"

Jill pulled the phone out of her purse. "Good idea." Once she hung up she said, "They're up for a break too. Just get off at the next exit."

Inside the restaurant the conversation was about the party and who would attend. It was then that Jill remembered to bring up her conversation with Sarah.

"Oh, Travis, I forgot to ask you! The other day I called Sarah. You know the girl with three daughters who I met in New York?"

"Sarah? Oh yeah, how are they doing?"

"Not good," Jill replied. "The aunt she was staying with was moved to a nursing home and they're foreclosing on her house. Sarah said she doesn't have a lot of options. So—I was wondering if your mom would have any kind of job for her either at the ranch or the bed and breakfast."

Travis sat for a few seconds, rubbing his chin. "Hmm—maybe—is she willing to move?"

"Yes, I already asked her that question, and she said, 'Home is where my children are.' So what do you think? Maybe we could buy them bus tickets so they can come to my graduation party, then your mom can meet them and see what she thinks."

Marge and Carol offered to chip in on the tickets, agreeing that it was a good idea. Then they waited to hear what Travis thought.

"Well," he finally replied after thinking it over, "I'll ask my Mom if Sarah and her daughters can stay at the bed and breakfast that weekend."

"Oh, Travis you're the best!" Jill replied happily. "That's a great idea! Okay…" Jill looked at her mom and Carol, then back at Travis. "We'd better head on down the road. We have a lot to do before the party."

Chapter 43

Once Bobby Sue and Bo agreed, Jill made arrangements for Sarah and the girls to take the bus from New York to Ohio, so they could arrive in time for the party and stay at the bed and breakfast. They were to arrive at the Columbus bus station at two o'clock on Friday afternoon. That would give Jill enough time to leave her parents' house and swing by the B&B to help get the rooms ready for their arrival, before picking them up.

***

Clara sat out on the front porch of the bed and breakfast hand embroidering a piece of linen when Travis walked up the steps to greet her.

"Hi, Grandma, what are you working on?"

Clara smiled. "Hello, dear. I'm working on another verse to frame, for one of the guest rooms here."

Travis nodded his approval as he looked over her shoulder to read what it said. *Be joyful always, pray continually, give thanks in all circumstances, for this is God's will for you in Christ Jesus. 1 Thessalonians 5:16-18.*

He smiled, "That's nice. It looks like it will be ready to frame once you finish the flowers."

Clara smiled. "I'm going to frame it to hang in the Thessalonians room. I was hoping to get it done before Jill's friend Sarah arrives."

"So that's where they're going to stay?"

Clara picked up her needle again. "Yes, that will be the room reserved for families. It's sixteen by twenty with an attached bathroom, and it overlooks the equestrian center. I thought the little girls would enjoy seeing the horses from the balcony off that room."

Travis sat down beside her. "That sounds perfect, Grandma. They really enjoyed the Clydesdales—you know—the ones I drove to the diner to find Jill. Maybe Mom would be able to use Sarah at the barn."

Clara continued to embroider, nodding in agreement. "That's a great idea." Travis looked at his watch and then back at the driveway.

"Jill should be here any minute. She wants to help get their room ready. She bought them a few small gifts that she wants to put in their room to welcome them."

Clara smiled as she paused from her needlework. "She's a nice girl. I really like her, Travis."

He patted his grandma's knee as he stood up. "I couldn't agree more, Grandma."

Chapter 44

Tara and Brad were on a break from their dance class. Brad wiped the sweat off his face and neck as he looked over at her. "Look at you! You're hardly sweating."

Tara smirked. "Yeah, well I must be in better shape than you!"

Brad wound up his sweat rag and flicked her with it.

Tara jumped. "Ew, Brad! That's disgusting. It's drenched with your sweat!"

Brad laughed. "Well, you're the cause of all this sweat, picking you up and tossing you in the air. Most of your dance moves are ballet and hardly take any effort at all."

Tara took her hand towel and started waving it in front of her face as she went into her character of Miss Dorcas, batting her eyes. "Yes, Benjamin, I'm a lady in waiting for a date. I must not perspire in front of a gentleman."

They both burst out laughing as he pulled her to sit down beside him. "Here's your date." He reached into his backpack, pulled out an apple, and offered it to her.

Tara looked at the apple and grinned. "Do you have any peanut butter in that knapsack of yours?"

Brad sighed. "As a matter of fact I do, Miss Dorcas. Would you like a knife too?"

She straightened her tee shirt as she once again batted her eyelashes at him. "Yes, please, and if you would be ever so kind and slice the apple for me, I would surely be grateful."

He shook his head. "Yes, Miss Dorcas. Would there be anything else you would like me to do for you?" Just then they heard the announcement saying their break was over.

Chapter 45

Jill paced back and forth in front of the bus terminal where Sarah and the girls were scheduled to arrive. She couldn't wait to see and hug them. Back at the bed and breakfast, Bobby Sue and Greta were preparing a light lunch for them. This would give Bobby Sue some time to determine how they could help with her situation.

Travis was startled when he heard Jill squeal. He looked up from his phone to see her run toward Sarah and the girls.

"Welcome to Ohio! Oh, I'm so glad to see you!" The girls were hopping up and down, as they tried to join in a group hug with Jill. Sarah wore a grateful smile when she saw Jill. Travis remained behind to let them calm down a bit, then he cleared his throat and joined the group.

Jill looked over her shoulder at him. "You remember my boyfriend, Travis—right?"

The girls nodded. "Hi, Travis!"

Sarah reached out to shake his hand. "Hi. Thank you so much for the bus tickets and making it possible for us to come!"

Travis shook her hand. "We're glad to help. Plus, this girl right here…" looking over at Jill, "had a big part in the process. Why don't we grab your bags and head out to the ranch? My mom and sister have made lunch for us."

Through misty eyes, Jill watched Sarah and the girls gather their bags and head to the truck. Her heart filled with joy and excitement for them and she could only wonder what wonderful things Jesus had planned for their future.

***

Everyone was busy back at the bed and breakfast, excited about the family's arrival. Clara had finished embroidering the flowers when she headed to the wood shop where Joe was making its frame.

Bo hauled in bags of ice to store in the freezer and stocked the refrigerator with cases of drinks. His truck was full of tables and chairs he had borrowed from the main house and the equestrian center. The forecast called for perfect weather for the weekend, so they were planning to set up tables and chairs in the flower garden, just outside the double glass doors of the Grand Room. Jack and Jake, from the college Bible study group, volunteered to hang speakers in the flower garden and create a stage for dancing.

Travis pulled up to the B&B at the same moment Clara and Joe walked toward the front porch. As they got out of the car, Travis gestured for his grandparents to come and meet Sarah and the girls.

Clara was the first to speak. "Welcome everyone! I'm Clara and this is Joe. We're Travis's grandparents."

Sarah stepped forward to shake their hands. Clara chuckled with delight. "Oh, come here!" She opened her arms and pulled Sarah into a big hug. "Around here we greet each other with hugs." Joe smiled and offered Sarah a shoulder hug, then warmly embraced each of the girls. Jill was the last in line to hug Clara.

Clara held on to Jill a little longer than the rest and whispered in her ear, "Hello, my pretty girl. You've been dearly missed around here."

Jill loved Clara's hugs. "I've missed you too."

Bobby Sue and Greta stood on the front porch and invited everyone into the garden area where lunch would be served. Sarah asked about their luggage.

Jill looked at Travis. "Do you mind bringing in their luggage?"

Travis started for the trunk of the car. "I'll set them inside the front door, then you can show them to their room after lunch."

Jill smiled at him. "Perfect! Thanks."

Everyone sat at the lunch table, including Jack and his brother. Greta had invited the brothers to eat with them since they had more than enough chicken enchiladas, as well as salad with homemade salsa, and chips. Bo offered to say the prayer, and the girls folded their hands as they had learned in New York.

"Dear Lord, we come to You with thanksgiving, not only for this meal, but for our friendship. There is a reason why we are all gathered here today and we ask that You open our minds, hearts and souls to seek Your desires. In Jesus' name, amen."

Everyone including Sarah, said amen.

Bobby Sue was full of questions for Sarah, including whether she had experience with horses, since she had heard she'd been comfortable around the Clydesdales in New York.

Sarah wiped her mouth with her napkin before she answered. "Yes, I have."

Nine-year-old Tessa spoke up. "My mama was a barrel racer."

Elisa, with a mouth full, chimed in, "Our daddy said she was the best that ever turned a barrel, and that's why he married her."

Sarah gave Elisa a quick, harsh look. "Elisa, what have I told you!"

Elisa's expression went from happy to sad in an instant. "Sorry, Mommy."

Sarah could feel the tension in the room as she cleared her throat and tried to soften her voice before addressing Elisa. "You know it's not polite to talk with your mouth full."

Then her youngest daughter of five, Aubrey, nodded her head and agreed with Sarah. "Yeah, it's not nice."

Chapter 46

After lunch everyone went their own way. Jill showed the guests to their quarter then offered them a tour of the homestead. After that they helped arrange tablecloths and carefully placed the decorations made by their mothers. Travis and his dad hung two bench swings from the front porch roof, one on each side of the doors. Then they placed several large flower pots by the edge of the walk, ready to be filled with fresh flowers. Clara was in the kitchen studying the menu and writing out a list of things to do before the big day. Joe was getting ready to put the final touches on the stage that Jack and his brother built.

While hanging the swings, Travis thought of all the little details that needed to be worked out regarding the merchandising of his dolls. He looked forward to talking this over with Jill, knowing she would be home all summer. It would give them an opportunity to see how well suited they were to working together. He also wanted her input on the outfits that would dress her mini-me doll. With her love for fashion, she would no doubt be good at that. He also planned to ask her to be a live model for the runway show and to be available at his booth to autograph the purchased dolls during a meet-and-greet for the customers.

His mind raced with more new ideas: Make a package deal with a creative short story book or bio to go with his adult dolls, and a coloring book to accompany his children's doll collection. He continued to think of other accessories he could design for the dolls: a scripture to scribe on the dolls' heart or maybe on the bottom of their feet. Create more role model dolls representing different character qualities that would encourage kids to look at their future with new hope. He couldn't wait until the party was over to have Jill all to himself to share the thoughts that consumed his mind.

***

Bobby Sue wiped the sweat from her brow then reached for her water bottle. "Whew, it's a bit warm out here."

Greta looked at her as she straightened up from leaning over a flowerpot. "It sure is." Then she glanced around and abruptly changed the subject. "Well, what do you think of Sarah?"

Bobby Sue replaced the cap on her water bottle. "Well, it's clear that she's under a lot of stress, by the way she reacted to the mention of their daddy. I don't think she was on the up and up about what really upset her."

Greta grabbed a bottle of water from the cooler. As she unscrewed the cap, she said, "Yep, I can't help but wonder where he is and why he would leave such a beautiful young family."

Bobby Sue nodded. "I'm going to talk with your dad tonight and see if we can offer her a room here at the bed and breakfast, just until we learn more about their situation and determine how we can help them." Greta was all for that idea.

Chapter 47

The party was in full swing, with music playing in the background, the buffet tables loaded, and family and friends gathered all around. Most of the older people sat at the tables in the Grand Room talking, while the young ones visited in the garden area. With the doors open and the ceiling fans on, it gave the Grand Room a cool, pleasant ambiance where the elders could mingle and still be a part of the celebration.

Brad, Jackie, and Tara arrived from Canton and sat at a table in the garden area with Jill, Travis, and Sarah. The girls were having the time of their life, dancing barefoot in the sundresses Jill bought them, with hair accessories to match. She gave Sarah a gift box of her favorite tea with a piece of Unique One jewelry—a leather bracelet with three silver initials spaced across it: T, E, A, representing each of her daughters' names. Jill had made it once she got home from New York and saved it to give to Sarah on a special Someday.

Even though it was Jill's celebration, she felt an underlying tug at her heart. She excused herself from the table to make a private phone call, a call that would change the course of her life. Walking back to the table in hopes she'd receive a confirmation call on her decision, she realized it was a new beginning for Sarah as well. Bobby Sue invited her to stay at the bed and breakfast for the summer.

This summer was holding a lot of surprising new beginnings. Tara was invited to stay in Canton as a paid actor along with Brad, appearing in the "Seven Brothers" musical. Sarah and her daughters were making their home at the Gunner's ranch, and Travis's doll collection was now in production. Then there was Jill's decision—would she live for love or risk love for her career; in the end would she love with faith and learn to have it all?

As the evening cooled off and the party lights glowed in the fall air, Brad and Jill prepared to take the stage and thank everyone for coming, then they would both give short speeches about their future plans.

Just as they neared the stage, Jill's phone rang, and she saw that the caller was her boss, Mr. Allen.

Jill took Brad's arm and pulled him close to her. "It's Mr. Allen. I need to take this call."

Brad shrugged and told her okay as he turned to take the stage.

Jill darted through the Grand Room and into a quiet corner before answering her phone. "Hello?" Moments later she returned with a letter in her hand. As she walked by Travis standing at the cake table she slipped it into his hand.

He looked confused. "What's this?"

Jill bit her lip, trying to stay composed. "This letter will explain what I'm about to announce. I'm sorry to do it this way, but I feel it's best for the both of us at this time in our lives." Then she turned and walked to the stage; putting on a stage smile, she took in a deep breath and grabbed the mic from Brad, joking, "Is it my turn yet?"

Everyone laughed as Brad smiled and took a bow. "You have the floor!"

Without hesitation she began, "To be perfectly honest I had a nice speech prepared but I just received a call from my boss, who's offered me a new, well-paid summer position, traveling from Tennessee to Chicago, then to New York, to lead seminars for new HR employees!" She continued. "How can a girl with a degree in hand refuse an offer like that? I said yes!"

Jill held back bitter-sweet tears that were welling up inside her as everyone applauded—except Travis who stared at her motionless.

Seeing the look on his face, Jill realized there was no turning back now. Travis knew that she had made a decision about their future: She had decided to risk love for her career.

Sitting by the pond, where he went when he needed to escape, Travis opened the letter.

Travis,

If you are reading this letter you know that I decided to take the job. I truly love you, and it pains me to write this knowing it will hurt you.

I knew it would be hard for me to follow through with the decision if I did it face to face. I'd give in and try to become the person you want me to be.

When talking to you about the future, I knew in my heart that I was not ready to fulfill your dreams about your becoming a father. Who knows, maybe someday I will be. But for now, I accepted this career opportunity because that's what I feel I'm confident in doing, starting a career.

I hope we can stay connected over the summer, to see how we feel over time.

Please consider everything I wrote in this letter as a small window to the confusion I've been wrestling with for awhile. I have to take this time to find out who I am before offering myself as a life partner.

All my love, Jill

***

Reflecting over Jill's story, you can see she is not ready for a committed relationship the way Travis is.

She is kind-hearted toward others and even toward children. The small seeds have been planted in, and through her life. These seeds are to show God's great love.

***

*As the story continues in "**Someday,**" we will see how the Sower's seeds blossom within this circle of friends from Ohio.*

❖ *What are the seed planters in Chapter 35? Are you letting God use you as a seed planter in your everyday life?*

❖ *In Chapter 39, Brad comforts Tara's nerves before her audition. Do you think he is starting to feel something for her, or is this his character? How does Tara interpret his actions?*

❖ *Do you see Jill's concern for Sarah and her three girls as part of a seed planter? Do you think the snowstorm in New York was a coincidence where they first met, or the start of "New Beginnings" for Sarah and her girls?*

❖ *Have you ever thought of displaying Bible scriptures throughout your home like Clara and Booby Sue did at the Bed and Breakfast? How do you think it would affect the atmosphere in your home?*

❖ *During Jill's celebration, being in a party atmosphere, surrounded by her family, and friends, she was not truly at peace. Have you ever felt sad or alone in a place filled with love and joy? How did you handle it?*

❖ *Her indecisiveness to follow her heart or follow her career weighed heavily on her the night of her graduation party. This was it, the decision that would direct her path to—New Beginnings. Do you feel she followed her desires, God's desire, or both?*

❖ *Do you feel Jill and Travis were not at the same stage in life when thinking of their future? What do you think about the letter Jill gave to Travis?*

***

Take notice of the small seeds planted in your life.

Journal daily, then you can look back, and see how His Hand,

the Sower, planted the people you come in contact with every day!

Don't miss the great opportunity to nurture the seeds planted in your life.

***

Thank you for taking time to read my novella!
I hope you've enjoyed it.
I would love to connect with you and hear your thoughts about it.
You can contact me at:

Authorsusanschmelzer@aol.com

(Facebook) Author Susan Schmelzer

Salvation is offered as a gift to us by God. The way to receive it is believing, accepting who Jesus is, and asking Him into your heart.

Romans 10:8-10 But what does it say? "The Word is near you, It is in your mouth and in your heart," that is, the Word of faith we are proclaiming. That if you confess with your mouth, "Jesus is Lord," and believe in your heart that God raised Him from the dead, you will be saved. For it is with your heart that you believe and are justified, and it is with your mouth that you confess and are saved.

***

Living out the knowledge of Scriptures and believing In It—is living by faith.

Hebrew 11:1 Faith is being sure of what we hope for and certain of what we do not see.

www.ingramcontent.com/pod-product-compliance
Lightning Source LLC
Chambersburg PA
CBHW060834120626
46557CB00001B/496
9781732759503